# Turk's Trading Post

## D.A. BARNHARD

PublishAmerica
Baltimore

First printing

All characters in this book are fictitious, and any resemblance to real persons, living or dead, is coincidental.

PublishAmerica has allowed this work to remain exactly as the author intended, verbatim, without editorial input.

Hardcover 978-1-4560-1256-4
Softcover 978-1-4560-1255-7
PUBLISHED BY PUBLISHAMERICA, LLLP
www.publishamerica.com
Baltimore

Printed in the United States of America

*To Don for having my cup of coffee ready every morning and along with Mike, Laurie and Barry, for bringing good times to the rest of the day.*

# Chapter One

Just one more bend in the river, that's bow the map read and that's how it was.

Turk halted the horse and the wagon came to a stop. Taking a good look around, he liked what he saw. He liked the look of the towering trees and the clean river. He even thought the air smelled very clean and fresh. Although he had never been near this place before, in a strange way it felt like home.

Turk carefully put the map back in it's leather pouch and took out his deed. It gave him such a proud feeling looking at the words. United States to John A. Turk 90 acres consideration of cash in the amount of 900 dollars. Recorded September I, 1848. Divided January 16, 1849.

The divided part went to his good mend Mr. Henry Dobbs, who Turk figured was just ahead of him on the trail. Not much of a trail, maybe not even a trail. He had been told, no one came to this part of the woods. No one wanted this property because it was too swampy. Turk had thought about it at length and he wanted it. The longer he thought about it, the more he wanted it. He imagined a rustic trading post built off the ground with a covered porch facing the small lake located close to the middle of the property People would come from miles around as it would save them from the long trip into town. Turk could not help smiling, he knew the post would be a success and he would have a good business and a better life. "You have to stop day-dreaming and move along," Turk told himself. Dobbs will be wondering what happened to me. He might wonder, but he wouldn't worry. He knew Turk could handle most anything that came his way. With another smile and a thoughtful look in his clear gray eyes, he got the horse moving on down the trail again.

Turk didn't get far when he smelled a campfire. He couldn't see the smoke, but the smell was there, mixed with something cooking. Maybe rabbit or squirrel or some other small animal. All he knew for sure is there would be beans. Dobbs always cooked beans. It made no difference if it was day or night, it didn't matter what else was cooking, there would be beans.

"Howdy, Turk," Dobbs yelled out. "About time you got here. Unhitch your horse and pull up a nice soft piece of ground and get ready for some good rabbit stew."

Turk got his strong sturdy body down from the wagon. He was hungry and it was a relief to stretch his legs.

Dobbs faithful dog came padding up to Turk and with a happy bark, let him know he was glad to see him too.

"Well, what do you think of it?" Turk asked after he had filled his plate and made himself comfortable.

"I think it's real purty here and it has a lot going for it, doncha think, Turk?" There's lots of timber around to build the trading post and lots of game and that little lake is plumb full of fish. I think I can catch them up in the shallows and get them with a pitchfork. I bet they would be real tasty too.

Dobbs had not shaved in days and the whiskers gave him a rugged look. His warm brown eyes were shining with excitement as he talked about his plans. He was older than

Turk , but he was just as strong and maybe even a little more determined to make this investment pay off.

The rest of the day was busy with unloading wagons and putting a kitchen of sorts together. They figured it would be better to keep the food in the wagons because of the stories they had heard about bears and wolves and even Indians, They made sure the horses were watered and tied where there was a nice patch of grass. The two men were special careful to secure the wagons. Many a settler had been awakened from a well-earned sleep to find their wagon had been on just enough of a grade that it had taken off on it's own.

It was decided the best place to sleep would be in their wagons for the time being. Turk and Dobbs were both ready for sleep as soon as it became dark.

Turk crawled up into his wagon and laid down on the worn mattress he had brought from home.

As he covered himself with an old quilt, he watched Dobbs and Old Dog crawl up in the other wagon.

"At least you have someone to keep you warm," Turk called out to Dobbs.

Dobbs didn't answer and Turk found he was not quite ready for sleep. He lay for a long time looking up at the stars and listening to the night sounds. He felt completely at peace. Just before dozing off, Turk became aware of a foul odor coming from the direction of the other wagon.

"Dobbs, you have been feeding that poor old dog beans again, haven't you? I swear, if you had a wall and if that wall had paint on it, Old Dog's farts would peel that paint right off!"

# Chapter Two

Slowly drinking coffee the next morning and watching Dobbs sipping on his cup while stirring the ashes of the campfire, Turk could see the ashes sticking to the whiskers on Dobbs weathered face and he knew his friend was doing some heavy duty thinking. He knew Dobbs well.

"Turk, doncha think them Indians who live here got cheated?" He finally asked.

"Well it don't happen too often, but when you are right, I guess you are right" Turk answered back. "It happened about ten years back that the U.S. Congress approved the so-called treaty of Washington that took thousands of acres from the Odawa Indians. The government bought it all for 16 cents an acre. They turned around and sold it to the first settlers for $1.25 an acre."

"Purty good profit and by the time we decided to buy, it was all the way up to ten dollars an acre." Dobbs sounded a little disgusted as he went on. "I guess it was the first chance for some to own their own land, so they figured it was a bargain. It must have been something when the early settlers saw their own land for the first time."

"Yep, Dobbs. I heard in town that when they came the

forest was filled with huge trees. Mostly white pine. Some up to 200 feet tall and about 8 feet around. There were deer, rabbits, beaver, a few bears and even fewer prairie chickens and lots of wolves. So many there is talk of putting a bounty on them. Imagine that, Dobbs, someday you might get paid for hunting!"

"You wouldn't be pulling my leg, would you, Turk?" Dobbs inquired with a big grin.

"I swear it's the truth. You could get paid for doing your favorite thing." Turk grinned right back. "That would be plumb wonderful, but I don't plan to start spending my fortune just yet. We better quit jawing and get to work. The trading post isn't going to build itself: you know." Dobbs threw the rest of his cold coffee on the ground. "Let's get busy."

The rest of the day was very busy. After a lot of talking and a little bit of arguing, they decided on the perfect building spot. Cutting down the sturdiest and straightest trees they could find, they sunk them deep into the swampy, wet ground. They kept adding pilings until they were sure the trading post would be high enough to stay above the snow melt and the Spring rains. At least they hoped they were sure. Neither men had ever built anything before, so nothing was for certain.

It was the hardest work either man had done for along time, but they didn't complain. They didn't even talk much. Each man knew what needed to be done and they knew they were building a future together.

Late in the afternoon, Dobbs was the first to say, "Let's rest. We don't have to do it all in one day."

Turk had been thinking along those same lines, but he felt a little proud that Dobbs was the one to make the suggestion. With a great sigh, he gently lowered his tired body to the ground He had an idea tomorrow morning he was going to have pain in parts of his body he never knew he had. He knew Dobbs would too. He also was sure that no one would even mention having any pain at all.

"Let's not get too fancy for supper. How do you feel about left-over stew?" Dobbs asked.

"You know I always eat anything you fix," Turk answered. "I don't like to cook and I don't say it often, but as long as I'm not complaining, you can figure I like your cooking about the same as I don't like mine." Turk knew he didn't have to praise Dobbs, but a pat on the back is nice once in a while.

After supper something happened that had never happened before and may never happen again. Dobbs and Turk both went sound asleep without cleaning their plates and slept right through until the sun woke them the next morning.

# Chapter Three

"It's a good thing hard work won't kill a person or we would have passed on weeks ago." Dobbs didn't exactly complain about the work, but he did manage to mention it a few times each day.

"We are making good progress though, doncha think, Turk?"

"Yep," Turk answered. "It's taking lots of trips into Muskie City for supplies and lumber and building materials, but we are getting there for sure. Would you like to have me draw a map of the town for you?"

Without waiting for an answer, Turk squatted down and selecting a stick, he began drawing in the soft dirt.

"Here is the main street and on the corner here is the bank. Next is a school that is sometimes a church. They have preachers that travel from town to town, so they never know for sure if there will be church or not. I heard sometimes they get together and just sing a few hymns. Across the street is the doctor's office. He is also the Justice of the Peace and sort of a dentist. A little farther down is the land office and the jail. The sheriff is there some of the time. The jail only has one cell, but that is not used much. They mostly use it when a rowdy has too much to drink in one of the two saloons in town. They built them right next to each other and the story goes that you can fall out of one and fall right into the other. I also heard that you would have better luck finding the sheriff in one of them rather than his office."

''I will have to check that out," Dobbs said with a chuckle. "Tell me more."

"I haven't been everywhere in town, but I think there is a cross street about here and a few of the town people live on that street. Mostly I go to the general store that has about everything. The couple who own it are very friendly and cheerful. Jessie is a little chubby, very short with white hair and has the rosiest cheeks and twinkling bright blue eyes. Her husband, Josh, is tall and thin, but with laughing blue eyes too. They are so proud of their store. As a matter of fact, they brag and tell you, if they don't have it, you don't need it.

There is a barbershop in a small add-on to the general store and the barber is also a sometimes dentist. Once in a while I'm getting supplies, when I hear strange noises coming from the shop. I wonder if someone is getting an extra close shave or maybe a tooth pulled."

"No, this isnt' right," Turk said laughing at himself. "That's what is so nice about drawing a map in the dirt, I can scratch out my mistake and do it over.

The bend in the street actually goes this way. Here is the post office and the livery stable and a feed mill. At the west end of town is the sawmill and lumber company. The Indian village is still further to the west, closer to the big lake. The village is always smoky and Josh told me it's because they burn smudge fires to try to keep fleas and mosquitoes away. They have a big problem with this because they use the dried skins of huge sturgeon fish on their wigwams to stay warm and dry."

"I'll have to go to town myself one of these days. I'm getting a little tired of looking at just your sorry face every day," Dobbs joked.

"I know exactly what you mean," Turk joked right back.

"Turk, doncha think this town is a lot like the one we came from," Dobbs asked.

"Yes it is," Turk answered. "Seems like the more things change, the more they seem the same." Turk had a thoughtful sound to his voice as he recalled the day he came to town and went into Dobb's store.

"I told you how the day before I had buried my mother and that I desperately wanted to get rid of the farm. I had known for a very long time that farming was not for me. You talked me into going to work for you in the store and it was the smartest thing you ever talked me into. Come to think of it, it was the only smart thing you ever talked me into. I loved the work. All of it. Stocking the shelves; the ordering; the customers. I even liked sweeping up after closing and looking around the store thinking about the next day.

I let it be known how anxious I was to sell the farm and everything with it. I told anyone who would listen that I would take the first decent offer and I did."

With all the talk of by-gone days, Turk had trouble falling asleep that night. He kept remembering the time before the farm had sold. He had good memories, but the ones keeping him awake was the bad ones.

He recalled how hard his pa worked every single day. It was back-breaking work. Often the weather would wipe out a crop and you would have to start over. It seemed like the work was endless. Turk tried to help out the best he could, but it was never ending. All day long, Turk would think about getting the work done and going into the house for supper.

Thinking back on the supper table was a good memory. Along with the good food, his mother always had a canning jar in the middle of the table. Sometimes filled with wild flowers or unusual looking weeds or even pine branches. This was by far the best time of his day. Once in a while there would be little ornaments stuck in the bouquet or even small pieces of candy.

Turk remembered exactly how his mother looked. She was small and had gray eyes and shiny black hair that she kept up in a tidy little bun. She moved very quietly and spoke softly and Turk loved her with all of his young heart. Turk always thought suppertime was her favorite time of the day too. There was laughing and talking and no hint of the bad time to come.

The bad time came the summer he turned fourteen. He woke that morning with the strange feeling something was wrong. Very wrong. He was shaking so much he had trouble getting dressed, but he knew he had to find out what was going on.

His mother was sitting quietly at the table, and had gotten so much older overnight. Something about the way she looked sent chills through him. Turk remembers feeling very frightened.

"Sit down, John." His mother said in a sad voice. "I have to tell you something. Your pa has gone away and he won't be coming back. John, he just couldn't take it anymore. The hard work has done him in. He has been talking about this for a long time, but he waited until you were old enough and big enough to take care of yourself and me. Before he left, he said, 'Tell old Turk that I love him and I'm proud of him, but there has to be more to life than this old farm and I'm going to find out what it is.'"

Turk remembers he had never been more frightened or more angry. He wasn't ready to take care of himself and he was sure he couldn't take care of his mother and certainly not the farm. He was mad at the world and the farm and especially his father. He was mad for four long years. He got stronger and kept the farm running somehow, but there was no joy in his life.

One sad day he found his mother sitting on the steps with tears on her cheeks that she seemed too tired to even brush away. She had taken off her wedding ring and as she held it up she spoke, "John I can't wear this anymore. I no longer have a husband. I don't feel married. If you want it, you may keep it. Maybe someday you will be able to look at it and remember the good days.

His mother was getting smaller and quieter by the day. She didn't cook anymore. There was no more flowers on the table, no more surprises. She mostly kept to her bed and slept. One sad morning, she didn't wake up.

Turk remembered how he dug her grave in a shady hollow and carved her name on a piece of wood. He stood for a long time looking at her grave and thinking how his mother used to be.

He couldn't know, but someone else was looking too. Close by, in some thick brush, a young girl with golden curls and dancing green eyes watched everything that he did. She lived on the adjoining farm and happened to be passing by. She thought he was about the handsomest boy she had ever seen. She knew he couldn't see her, but she was blushing. She watched as he took an old canning jar and filled it with wild flowers. He gently placed the jar in front of the little piece of wood. After a long while, he lifted his chin and straightened his shoulders and sadly walked away.

The young girl watching thought her heart was going to break. The tears filled her green eyes, but she was afraid to wipe them away. She couldn't bear the idea that he might see her and know she had seen everything. She didn't move until she was sure she would not be found out.

The old sad memories haunted Turk through the long night and in the morning he was more tired than when he had gone to bed.

After coffee and a little breakfast, Turk decided a nice warm bath is what he needed to wash away the old sad memories.

Talking about the merits of taking or not taking a bath, Dobbs asked Turk, "Doncha think we are about ready to open up this trading post for business?"

"Yep. We are as ready as we are ever going to be," Turk answered. "At least I will be clean and neat for the grand opening."

# Chapter Four

"I sure hope that neat and clean comment was not a shot at me and I really hope you didn't mean Old Dog," Dobbs muttered. Dobbs idea of a bath was a quick jump in the little lake with a bar of soap. Turk would heat water on the cook stove and linger in the big washtub until the water turned cool. Old Dog had no idea at all. The only way he was going to get wet is by getting caught outside in a sudden downpour.

"I'm sorry, I guess I'm a little out of sorts this morning," explained Turk. "I apologize."

"I accept your apology, but I don't know about this dog. He's not as sweet and understanding as me." Dobbs had to laugh as he said this and Turk couldn't help but join in.

As it turned out both men were more than ready, clean and neat, and eager for the post to open. The opening was a great success. Lumberjacks, settlers and Indians all were curious and they were glad to shop at the post, saving themselves the long trip into Muskie City. Jessie and Josh came from town and complimented the men. They were surprised that so much work had been done in a short amount of time. One of the surprises was learning they had done so well at stocking exactly what their customers would want.

A few days later it was a perfect day to relax on the open porch, sitting on one of the comfortable benches that Dobbs had made.

It was a perfect midsummer morning. Rain had come in the night and turned the maple leaves and white pine branches a silver shimmer in the early sunlight. The little lake had a shimmer of it's own. It was a scene that the men would not soon forget.

Turk was enjoying his coffee and drinking in the beauty of the morning. He placed his cup down beside him and clasping his big hands together, he stretched them in front of him and then over his head, finally cradling the back of his head. With his hands still together he looked up at the sky and thought about how much better his life was compared to the old days.

His thoughts were interrupted by the sound of Dobbs shuffling around the corner of the porch, talking to the Old Dog as usual.

"Yep, I need a cup of Turk's coffee. That will get me going." There was no response from the dog and Dobbs would have been truly surprised if there was.

Turk nodded to his friend and Dobbs nodded right back. Old Dog gave some kind of a woof sound and flopped down at Turk's feet.

"Sit yourself down and just look at this morning. You have to admit it is really something," Turk quietly added.

"You are right about that. I have been sitting over in my lean-to thinking the same thing. We sure found ourselves a little bit of Heaven right here on Earth, doncha think, Turk?"

Turk took another swallow of coffee and nodded his head in agreement.

The two old friends sat together in the kind of silence you have when you have known each other so well for so long.

Dobbs, deciding he had been quiet long enough, started to talk about all that had happened over the past few weeks. "We did so good with the trading post, I'm thinking we are going to get rich. We better make some plans on how we can spend our money. Maybe we should plan a big trip somewhere. How about France or England or maybe the moon?"

"Whoa there, Dobbs, I don't want to go anywhere and how did you figure on getting to the moon?"

"I know you won't agree with me," Dobbs answered, "but I do think someday it will be possible and men will even walk on it."

"You better just drink your coffee and rest your poor old tired brain," Turk said with a chuckle. Another companionable silence was broken by the sound of someone coming down the path from the river.

"It must be an Indian," Turk ventured. "I'm sure all the loggers went up river on another run. Those men about run us out of supplies when their river shanty pulled up and they came in to shop. I'm still amazed at all the tobacco and especially all the hard candy they bought. I didn't know big tough loggers liked candy so well."

"I have a list started for more supplies," Turk mentioned. "Take a look and see if you have anything to add."

"I sure have," Dobbs replied. "I need more board's and nails and I'm starting to run a little short on beans."

"We can't have that," Turk said with a grin.

"Why it's that ole Chief Crafty coming to do more trading. I don't call him that to his face, I just call him Chief. He seems to like that," Dobbs added. "He pretends he doesn't speak much English and understands less, but that's not so. He is a slick trader. The only problem being he has met one just a little slicker!"

19

"Howdy, Chief," Dobbs called out.

The Indian held up a bundle of furs and a couple of beautiful woven baskets. His brown skin shown in the morning sunlight. His black hair and dark eyes complete the picture. He stands straight and tall as he quietly speaks only one word, "Trade."

"Good, Chief," Dobbs said as he stood too. "Let's go in and do some trading. I hope you take it easy on me this time. The other day you took advantage of me something awful."

Turk couldn't hear after they went inside, but he was sure there was some powerful trading going on and just as sure that somehow Dobbs would come out ahead.

# Chapter Five

Muskie City was growing. Turk was always surprised at the many changes. There were new businesses and new homes. The settlers were glad to buy land at the bargain prices from the government and were happy to farm their new land, but many wanted to live in town or close by. They felt they needed the community with all the comforts that provided. The doctor, the bank, the stores and especially close neighbors.

All of this was not true for Turk. Dobbs and Old Dog was all the company he wanted. He liked the days when the post was not busy and there was not a lot of people around, but he did enjoy his days in town too. He looked forward to picking up supplies and especially getting all the local news.

"Hello, Josh," Turk called out to his friend who was busy setting up some kind of a hat display. "Are you going to have a big sale on hats?"

"Oh, no," Josh answered. "We don't have sales because my merchandise is a better buy than you can find anywhere."

Turk figured this was true. As far as he knew, Jessie and Josh's general store was the only one in town.

"Here is my supply list and while you are getting it together, I sure would appreciate it if you would let me in on what's been going on in town and anything else you figure I ought to know." Turk was sure this would bring Jessie out of the backroom as telling gossip was one of her joys.

She gave Turk a big bear hug and said, "You are looking just as handsome as the last time you were here. Let's see where should I start?

We now have a hardware store and a couple of new homes and of course, our fancy new boarding house. Most of all, you must meet May, the owner. She is definitely one of a kind."

Jessie's looks were changing as she talked. Her blue eyes were twinkling, her cheeks were getting a little rosy and she seemed about ready to burst with excitement.

"Calm down, Jessie," Josh jokingly told his wife. "Turk's already said he has some time so you don't need to pitch a fit over it!" While they were laughing over Josh's comment, they heard the door open and a woman sauntered in. Not just any woman, but someone special.

"May, we were just now talking about you," Josh managed to say.

"I am sure it was something most flattering, but don't tell me what it was," May was smiling as she said this. "If it was real good, I would love it and if it was bad; I wouldn't believe it. Oh my, looks like you have a customer that made it here before me. Who is this good-looking gorgeous man?"

"I would like you to meet Miss May Stone, our newest resident," Jessie made the introductions in a grand manner. "She owns the boarding house and she is a busy lady."

Turk took her offered hand and politely said, ''How do you do, Maam?"

May couldn't resist grabbing him in a big hug. Before letting him go, she said, "Let's get this straight right now. I'm not Maam or Miss Stone, I'm May. Who might you be?"

"Well my given name is John A. Turk, but folks call me Turk," Turk answered after he caught his breath.

"Not me," May laughed, "I will call you Johnny. You are way too handsome to be someone called Turk. As a matter of fact, you are the best thing I've seen in this town. No offense, Josh."

Josh quickly replied, "None taken"

All kinds of thoughts were going through Turk's mind. Suddenly the store was filled with new sights and sounds and even smells. May was a big woman. But not too big and she carried herself well. Her flowery hat was perched upon her pinned up bleached blond hair that had started coming loose and fell in curly strands around her shoulders. Her rose colored satin outfit rustled as she moved. Her makeup and perfume was applied with a heavy hand, but it looked good on her. She was like a happy colorful tornado.

"How long are you going to be in town?" May asked in a friendly voice.

"I'm not sure," Turk answered. "Sometimes I'm here for the day and sometimes I stay overnight."

"I have a grand idea, Johnny." May said suggestively. "I make the best chicken and dumplings in the country and I have the most comfortable beds in town. Why don't you come for supper and spend the night?"

For the first time in his life, Turk knew how it felt to be dumbfounded. He didn't answer. He just stood there and didn't say a word.

"Think it over," May said matter of factly. "The offer stands. Here's a list of stuff I need, Josh." With a toss of her curls and a rustle of her skirt, she sashayed out the door, but not before turning and looking right at Turk, she gave a slow deliberate wink!

Jessie and Josh couldn't help it, they both broke into a fit of laughter. When Josh could finally speak, he said, "You should see your face, Turk! What on earth are you going to do?"

Finding his voice, Turk said in a firm quiet way, "First I'm going in the backroom and see if the barber is there. I need a shave and a haircut and get spruced up some. I guess I'll spend the afternoon looking over the town. I want to go out to the Indian village and get some of those clever baskets they make. What time do you reckon supper is served?"

"I think around six," Jessie said with a smile.

"I need to tell you something," Josh tried to be serious. "Do not offer May any money. She might throw you out in the street. Buy her a little gift of some kind. So, this means you are taking her up on her offer."

Turk turned around with a big grin on his face, "It sure does look like that's exactly what I intend to do, doncha think?"

# Chapter Six

Leaving the barbershop and climbing into his wagon, Turk realized he could do whatever he liked and had the whole afternoon all to himself. He stroked his smooth fresh-shaven face and could smell the flowery scent on his hands from some stuff the barber had splashed on him. He was sure hoping the fresh air would get rid of the smell.

Turk couldn't help feeling a little guilty and sort of lazy. He couldn't remember when he had last had a store bought shave and had his hair cut by someone other than Dobbs.

"Oh well," Turk muttered to himself, "this is kind of a special day for me and I've always wanted to explore this town a little better. Seems like the perfect day to do just that."

Driving down main street, he noticed many new buildings. They were easy to spot because the wood didn't have that old familiar weathered look. Here and there you could see a bit of colorful paint, but mostly plain gray wood. There was a new boardwalk with a few benches scattered about. It appeared most of these benches were being used by the old men of the town. Turk smiled as he thought how Dobbs would feel right at home. Dobbs was especially good at sitting and even better at keeping up with the tall tales the men were certainly telling.

Turk checked out the side streets too. He saw many new settler's homes and more than a few gardens. The gardens were well tended and full of vegetables of all kinds. Not very many flowers. Busy settlers didn't have much time for unnecessary plantings.

Turk figured he would probably never live in a town, but if he did, this one might not be too bad.

Everyone was so friendly and most waved at Turk as he drove slowly by.

Outside of town, he drove by the busy sawmill. Without a doubt, the busiest place around. Everyone needed lumber. A growing town had use of lumber and building materials. No wonder the owner, Mr. Scutter, had the fanciest house in town and Turk was pretty sure he was the richest man around and getting richer every day.

Quite a ways beyond the sawmill was the Indian village. Even before Turk was close, he could see the smoky haze and smell the fishy, smoky odor. He knew that was the way it was and always would be. He didn't mind and he drove right into the middle of the village. He stopped when he spotted the Indian that came to the post once in awhile. Small Indian children came close to see what this white man wanted.

Climbing down from the wagon, Turk used gestures to let Chief Crafty know that he wanted eight large baskets and six smaller ones. After a little haggling, they came to an agreement. Each man figured the deal was fair. As he was leaving he spied a very unusual basket. It was smaller on top and had a wide bottom. The color was different, a shiny brown color. He didn't want to appear anxious, but he decided the basket would make a perfect gift for May. Dobbs would have been proud of the way Turk handled the whole deal. He left with the basket and with Chief Crafty thinking Turk had done him a big favor by taking that odd basket off his hands.

Heading back toward town, Turk could tell by the sun and by his stomach it was getting close to suppertime. He drove the wagon to the livery stable and unhitched his uncomplaining horse. He knew the stableman would take good care of the horse and the baskets would still be there in the morning.

"I'm taking this one basket with me," Turk yelled back at the man. "It's going to be a special present for a friend." Turk had a plan.

He found the closest saloon and asked the bartender for his finest bottle of whiskey. He had to go to the backroom to fetch it. The bottle was so dusty and looked like it had been around a long time. He paid for the bottle and left the saloon thinking that the good stuff was not sold often.

The bottle fit neatly into the clever little basket and looked as nice as Turk expected it would.

When he arrived at the boarding house, May thought so too.

"Oh Johnny," May gushed. "I love it. I know exactly what to do with the whiskey and after the whiskey is gone, I have a perfect plan for the basket." She gave Turk a hug and a playful wink, "You sure know how to treat a lady."

Having fed her three boarders earlier, she rushed them out of the dining room and began fixing the table up fancy with candles and fine dishes not normally used. "Sit right down at the head of the table." May cheerily told Turk. "Make yourself at home and get ready for something good."

May carried a big bowl of chicken and dumplings and put it smack dab in the middle of the table. She filled tall glasses with wine and the meal began. It was all very good. He didn't know what was the best, but one thing he did know was his wine glass never went empty.

As May cleared the table, she said, "Go find yourself an easy chair in the sitting room. This won't take long and then we can get started on that bottle of fine whiskey. We can drink and talk at the same time."

Usually Turk was not much for talking. He was content to let Dobbs handle that, but he soon found out May was interested in what he had to say, so he kept on talking.

"I don't normally talk so much," Turk apologized.

May gave a little giggle and told Turk, "I do have a way with men. They get very relaxed and friendly around me."

Turk wondered if maybe the drinking had something to do with that.

Soon he found himself telling May about the farm and how his Pa took off and how he was so angry for a long, long time. How he hated the world and growing up so fast. How his mother gave up and slowly wasted away. He told her it made him so sad. He felt like he had let his beloved mother down.

"This is strange, I don't remember talking about this before. Or at least not for a long time," Turk admitted.

May refilled their glasses again and slowly said, "I can top your sad story, Johnny, I don't usually talk about this either and I won't give you all the details, but I had to grow up fast too. My folks died and my brother and me had to find new homes. My brother made out pretty good, but I kept being shuffled from one place to another. I was either worked to death or there was always some dirty old man after me. I was only fifteen and I knew it was time for me to take care of myself. I had no choice.

For six long hellish years I lived in an awful room above a saloon in town. I slept with so many men I lost count. Some good men, but some angry mean ones who thought treating a woman rough was part of the bargain. I was beaten and had lots of black eyes. Big chunks of my hair was pulled out and sometimes the Doc would have to stitch me up. I would heal and go back to work. The only thing that kept me going was to save every penny I could and my dream of leaving that terrible place and opening up a boarding house."

May took a big swallow from her glass before going on. "I also made a vow to myself that when I could leave, from that time on, I would decide if I wanted a man and who that man would be."

The next thing that happened and not knowing how he got there, Turk found himself in May's fancy bedroom.

"I know you boys are partial to your long underwear, but try on that nightshirt that's on the edge of the bed. See if you like it." May gave Turk a slow wink, "I think you will."

The soft material felt good against Turk's bare skin. He did like it very much.

Just then, May pulled the covers back and Turk couldn't help exclaiming, "Damn, I never saw such pretty red sheets much less slept on them."

"Well, I'm not sure how much sleeping you are going to get, but I'm glad you like them. Hell, that's just one more of the promises I made to myself," May said sadly. "When things got really bad, I would dream of red silk sheets."

May had learned her trade well. She knew every way to give a man pleasure and how to have some fun herself at the same time. She was right about Turk not getting a lot of sleep, but when he finally drifted off it was with knowing he was a completely satisfied man.

In the morning as Turk was taking off the soft nightshirt he was liking more and more, May hollered up the stairs, "When you get decent, come down and have a cup of coffee before you leave. No civilized man should start his day without a cup."

May and Turk said their good-bys like good true friends. It was all natural and right, but Turk guessed he had a swagger in his step as he went to the stable to get his horse and wagon. Taking care of the bill, he made his way to the general store.

"Howdy," Turk called out as he sauntered in.

Like always, Jessie and Josh stood together behind the counter. This morning was just a little different Turk knew they were itching to find out what happened.

"Tally up my account while I load these boxes," Turk said as he stated carrying supplies out to the wagon. He was not surprised to see Josh right behind him, but he had an excuse.

"By the way, there are some letters I tucked in one of your boxes that the postmaster bought over to the store," Josh explained. He said to tell you to check for mail once in a while.

"I didn't expect anyone would be writing to me," Turk wondered out loud. "Who could it be?"

"It's a woman," Josh offered. "I happened to notice."

His curiosity aroused, Turk fished out the letter and checked the return address. "It's not a woman. It's a little girl named Hester Lee from back home who used to hang around Dobb's store an awful lot. I used to wonder if she didn't have better things to do, but I guess she didn't because she was there almost every day. Maybe she just liked Dobb's big stories."

"You sure get a lot of attention from females it seems to me," Josh pointed out.

Turk was certain there was more Josh wanted to say, but he couldn't quite get up the nerve to do so.

Paying his bill in full and picking up the last box from the counter. Turk turned as if to leave. Halfway to the door he stopped and turned around and said, "Alright I'm only going to say this one time, so listen good." Jessie and Josh stood so still and it was easy to see they were holding their breath. Turk continued in a firm calm voice, "I have to be completely honest. That was the very best, grandest chicken and dumplings supper I ever had!"

# Chapter Seven

The next day back at the post the early morning stillness was broken by Dobb's hearty laughter when Turk told him how he had put Jessie and Josh in their place.

"I would have liked seeing the look on their faces," Dobbs added. "Doncha think you were a little hard on them?"

Dobbs got an even bigger chuckle out of the rest of the story. Turk explained that he liked to stop on the little hill outside of town and look back at Muskie City nestled in it's own little valley. As he gazed around, he let go with a big sudden laugh himself. It was so big and sudden that it frightened Old Horse into doing some fancy side-stepping and Turk had to grab the reins and calm him down. Behind May's boarding house hanging on the clothesline and flapping in the breeze for all the town to see was the prettiest red silk sheets you ever saw!

This started Dobbs off on another round of laughter. After he had wiped his eyes on his shirt sleeve, he announced that he figured Turk and Old Horse both better stay home for a while. That might be the only way to stay out of trouble.

The two old friends drank their morning coffee and planned their day. The chores were divided almost evenly. Dobbs took care of most of the outside chores and Turk kept busy running the trading post Turk did wander outside sometimes and did some garden work or check on the animals. Once in a while Dobbs would come in to the post and jaw with certain customers. He had his favorites. They had busy days, but their best days were the ones spent fishing or hunting. Even a day spent cutting wood was a welcome change.

The rare times they were both busy elsewhere, they left a clever sign on the door stating; Not here, close by, ring bell. The old bell hung over the door did not ring very often.

Dobbs did most of the cooking and he was pretty good at it too. Turk thought he cooked beans more often than necessary, but he didn't complain. Sometimes he even guessed Dobbs threw in an extra handful to see if Turk would say something.

"How do you feel about starting work on the root cellar today?" Dobbs asked in a voice that meant he had already made up his mind. "I found the perfect spot for it."

"Sure, glad to help as soon as I get the supplies put away," Turk volunteered. "I need to sharpen my shovel and pick and I'll be raring to go."

The rest of the day was spent on the root cellar. It was going to be about eight foot square with a six foot ceiling with strong timbers reinforcing the dirt walls and also the ceiling. The floor was made up of flat stones gathered from the river's edge. They only stopped long enough to wait on two settlers that came in for a couple of things. The two men worked steadily until it started to get dark.

As they cleaned their tools before putting them away, Turk remarked, "You know, I think we have a good chance of getting this done before bad weather."

"Sure we will," Dobbs said with a smile in his voice. The hardest part will be the door. It will have to be strong enough to keep the wild animals out and simple enough for you to be able to open it and me too of course."

Still smiling, Dobbs commented, "It should be ready just in time to fill it with all the good vegetables from the garden. I can almost taste the rabbit stew with potatoes and cabbage or maybe I'm just getting hungry. You forgot to feed me today, Turk."

While it was still light enough to read, Dobbs read the letters from Hester Lee "That Hester Lee sure does write a nice letter, doncha think, Turk?"

''I'll take your word for it," Turk answered. "I'm not much on letter reading or letter writing either."

Dobbs was still reading when he said, "Imagine this, Hester Lee and her aunt are making clothes on a sewing machine contraption and even with two machines they have trouble keeping up with the demand. The machines are faster and do a much better job. That Hester Lee is smart and especially pretty too, donch a think, Turk?"

"I guess, I never really thought about it," Turk answered.

Dobbs thought to himself: I'm sure that's true, but I know for a fact she has thought about you for a long time and someday she just might do something about it.

# Chapter Eight

There was really no way to tell. Was it the sun shining on the hatchet clenched in Dobb's hand that he was waving like a wild man or the wicked gleam in his eyes that frightened the young Indian boys away?

Dobbs had left the trading post early that morning just as the sun began to rise. After telling Turk about the letter he had written to Hester Lee back home and making sure he knew he should mail it the next time he went to Muskie City for supplies.

"I understand," Turk told his old friend, "Seems like a real fat letter. You must have had a lot to say."

"Well, by now you should have figured out that I always have a lot to say. Now I'm off to do battle with as many dead trees as I can find I'll be taking a jug of water with me and some of those good old hard biscuits. I doubt if they will break apart even if I carry them in my pocket. I won't be back until suppertime. I'm off. My saw and hatchet are ready and so am I. Look out trees, here comes Dobbs!"

The early Fall nights required at least a small fire and there was always something cooking on the stove. It would not be long before Winter settled in. Turk and Dobbs had heard more than a few stories about Michigan winters. The old-timers swore they could tell if it was going to be a hard winter and if there would be a lot of snow. For some odd reason it was important to know if Muskie River would freeze completely over and especially good to know how thick the ice was going to be. Both men decided the winter was to be what it was going to be. No more. No less.

Firewood was not hard to find Many trees had succumbed to last winters cold and the Spring winds. Dobbs busily worked his way around the small lake making piles of cut wood along the way. He would hitch up both horses to the wagon and collect the wood some other day. This day he would cut as much as he could and he guessed that would be a good day's work.

Dobbs was feeling good. "I can still do a fair day's work," he said out loud to himself. "I might be considerable older than Turk. But I can work right along side him and never slow up." He didn't slow up. Dobbs kept the steady pace going all morning.

Sometime later he looked around and realized he had left the lake behind and was now on the south side of the river. Slowly he began hearing soft voices and little giggles.

The three small Ryerson girls were on the other side of the river picking berries. They looked just as they did when they came to the post with their folks. They would be dressed in brightly colored sun-bonnets and aprons and they were wearing those same colorful clothes now. The colors made them easy to see, but they had no idea Dobbs was on the other side watching them.

It seemed the day became even more pleasant and about that time, Dobbs spied another group of downed trees. He started right in with his busy cutting thinking this day is turning out just fine.

As often happened, Dobbs was lost in his own little world. His hands were busy and so was his imagination. Mrs. Ryerson will be making jam with those berries and maybe pies. He could almost taste the warm sweet pie. I better stop and have a biscuit. I'm suddenly hungry. If I try real hard maybe I can make myself believe it has jam on it.

Suddenly, or maybe it had been going on a while, he heard different sounds from across the river.

Loud shouts and whoops and some in-between crying. He couldn't make out exactly what was going on, but he knew the little girls was in trouble.

Hurrying down to the riverbank, he saw at once what was taking place.

Two young Indian boys who were not much older than the girls were terrorizing the helpless scared little girls who were holding on to each other and trembling with fright. The boys were swinging long sticks and circling and acting like they meant to hit them. The smallest girl tripped and fell to her knees. This brought on louder cries and Dobbs decided he had to do something.

He found a place in the river where rocks made a sort of path and grabbing his hatchet be jumped in the water yelling with all his might.

"You get to hell out of here, you raggedy heathen cowards," Dobbs screamed in his meanest voice. The boys took off and never looked back. Dobbs heard them crashing through the brush and figured at the very least, they would end up with some pretty good scratches and bruised egos. Dobbs guessed they had a canoe nearby and were now headed back to their village where they would stay for a while.

After the girls calmed down and picked up the spilled berries, they all sat down on the ground. The girls were starting to get their smiles back and were getting over their fright. Dobbs slowly realized he must look bad with his whiskers and matted hear with wood chips clinging to his sweaty face. He couldn't control a small chuckle and finally a really loud belly laugh as he realized he was surely scarier looking than the Indian boys could ever hope to be. The little berry pickers found themselves laughing too.

"You girls hurry on straight home," Dobbs said after the laughter died down. "I will keep an eye on you until you are out of sight."

As he watched, the notion came to him that he might get a pie or a jar of jam out of this. If he was really lucky, he might get both.

# Chapter Nine

"I'm sure looking forward to supper tonight," Turk remarked. It will be so good to have beef instead of wild game for a change. It was sort of lucky in a way that Ryerson didn't have anything to trade except a young heifer he didn't need or want and he traded a quarter of it for supplies he did need. Good trade all around. Both parties satisfied.

Dobbs nodded his head in agreement He was nearly always happy with Turk's trading skills, but deep down he fancied himself the better trader. He also knew Turk was getting to be a sharper trader all the time.

The Fall weather had moved in the last few days and the two men were kept busy harvesting their fine garden. They were pleased and a bit surprised the soil was so rich as they had been led to believe the ground would be too swampy to be any good. The root cellar was full of potatoes, cabbage, winter squash and a few parsnips and beets. Time would tell if the cellar was cool and dry enough to keep food and if it was even a good idea at all.

The men were a little concerned about the horses and the chickens. They were able to buy corn and hay from a nearby settler and some from the livery in town. Dobbs had decided he would build a small fire in the stove in the lean-to attached to the barn when the really frigid weather hit. He had informed Turk he would be moving into the post when the weather turned cold. Dobbs had not mentioned Old Dog yet, but he figured Turk would want the dog to stay warm too. Dobbs also guessed Turk would probably think a bath for both dog and man would be in order. He thought that was a bridge that could be crossed when they came to it.

"Good thing we found that spring near the edge of the lake, doncha think, Turk? Nobody will go thirsty and I'm bettin' it flows all winter long. It's good water and it's cold too."

"That was a good find," agreed Turk. "Speaking of the lake, I think we should give it a name. My name is on the post, so I think we should call it Lake Dobbs."

Dobbs broke out in a big grin. "That's a really good idea, but I have a better one," Dobbs grin got even bigger. "Everyone knows who Turk and Dobbs are, so I think a good name would be Lake Henry. Someday when we are dead and gone, people will wonder, 'Who on earth is Henry?'"

"I agree," Turk said with a chuckle in his voice. "It will give everyone something to talk about."

The rest of the day was spent getting both wagons ready to go to town the next day. They had figured it would take at least two wagons fully loaded with supplies to make it through the long, cold winter. They would not be going to Muskie City again after the snow started.

Turk had prepared Josh at the general store on the last trip. He told him to order extra and Josh had many helpful suggestions on what he figured the post would need. Both men realized the settlers in the wilderness would be depending on the post for their necessities. First was food, but a close second would be guns and shells. If something went wrong with a settler's gun, it would be disaster. No one lasted long in the wilderness without a gun.

This first winter would be mostly trial and error. Josh had experience on what would be needed and everyone agreed the best thing to do would be stock what they could and hope they made the right choices.

The evening found Turk and Dobbs relaxing on the porch after their tasty beef roast supper drinking their customary after supper coffee. As they looked out over the small lake, it was as if both men had the same notion at the same time. Both men raised their cups and holding the cups out toward the lake. In one voice they proclaimed, "Here's to you Lake Henry."

# Chapter Ten

The lantern shone just enough light to harness the horses and hitch them to the wagons. The trip about three hours if everything went well, so Turk and Dobbs knew if they wanted to make it in one day, everything must go perfect and they needed an early start.

"I wondered if Old Dog was coming along, but I see he has already picked out his spot next to you," Turk inquired.

"If I go., most often Old Dog goes too," Dobbs answered. "He will ride a while, then walk some and probably do a lot of sniffing and checking things out along the way. I'm taking some jugs of water and some of those hard biscuits you are so fond of, just in case we need them."

Like all good backwoods men there would be a set of tools under the driver's seat for wagon repairs. No one wanted to break down on the trail. You may wait a long time before help came along.

The two men took off in the dark, but it wasn't long until the sun came up. They could feel the welcome warmth on their backs and soon all over their bodies.

As they rode in silence, Turk was thinking about the list of supplies. Coffee for sure and some foods like dried apples and prunes because they would last for a time. A couple of rifles and shotguns. Some gloves and socks and extra coal oil and as many candles as he could get.

After about two hours, Turk noticed Dobbs slowing down a bit. "Want to stop and stretch our legs?" Turk hollered back to Dobbs.

"Sounds like a plan to me," Dobbs answered. "Bouncing around in this wagon is a little hard on the kidneys. I guess I'll let some out and then grab one of those jugs and put some more back in."

Turk jumped down from his wagon and nodded at Dobbs as he and his dog took off through the brush. Turk took off on the other side of the trail and took care of his needs too.

The second half of the trip was a lot warmer and soon they were coming down the rise outside of town and Muskie City lay before them.

Pulling up alongside the boardwalk in front of the general store, both men bounded from their wagons at about the same time.

Looking around, Dobbs remarked, "This here town plumb amazes me. I don't make it here often and when I do, it's hard to believe all of the new buildings and all the people."

"Yep," Turk agreed. "I will let Josh know we are here so he can start tilling our order. I also need to go to the bank and get some savings so we can settle up with the store for the year. We probably have a few outstanding bills and I think it's important to take care of them.

"You do your thing and I'll do mine," Dobbs offered. "I'll be going to the post office to mail a letter to Hester Lee and I imagine I will have two or more from her waiting for me. First let's get some water for our horses. Can we take them to the stable and get some there?"

"Sure enough," Turk answered his old pal. Leave it to Dobbs to make sure the animals were taken care of.

After their wanderings, Turk was the first to make it back to the store.

As Josh tilled the boxes with supplies, he was bringing Turk up-to-date on all the news. "Such big news. I don't know just where to start." Josh was excited. "First off, May bought up all the land to the east of town. Her property line butts right up next to yours. She plans to build a Park and sell lots to settlers for building homes. She found out lots of them don't really want to live in town, but close enough that they can take advantage of all the town offers."

"I guess the boarding house business must be real good," Turk managed to get a quick word in.

"And it's going to get better," Josh said with a sly look on his face. "There is a railroad coming to Muskie City. May told me they contacted her and reserved rooms for their workers for all winter. I didn't know they could lay track in the winter, but I guess they can. This will be a big project, probably a couple of years."

Turk was getting interested, "Where will this railroad be?"

"Wouldn't you know," Josh paused for effect. "Between Scutters Lumber Mill and the Indian reservation. So that means that old man Scutter will just keep on getting richer and richer."

"Sounds like this town is going to keep on growing," Turk said with a grin. "Hope no one figures out there is enough growth to warrant another general store."

Josh rubbed his chin thoughtfully, "Wouldn't surprise me. I reckon I have enough loyal customers to keep me going. Jessie don't eat much anymore and we are not used to high living. We should be alright."

Dobbs got back in time to help Josh and Turk load the wagons. During the loading, Josh winked at Turk and told him, "That special item you ordered is wrapped in brown paper at the bottom of the box of socks and gloves."

Turk nodded his head to let Josh know he understood.

Climbing into the wagon, Turk remarked, "You know, I wonder why the trip back to the post always seems so much longer?"

As he waved so long, Josh had the last word, "That's easy. You don't have my handsome smiling face to look forward to. Have a good winter, boys and remember to be careful. You are pretty much on your own back at the post. I'll be looking for you in the Spring."

# Chapter Eleven

The post was a welcome sight. The trip home was uneventful, but still a long, long trip. It was starting to get dark and there was a chill in the air.

"I wouldn't have a problem with driving these wagons into the barn and unloading them in the morning," Turk offered.

Dobbs answered right away said, "I'll vote for that. I will unhitch the horses and take care of them if you want to get a fire going and fix a pot of coffee and maybe rustle something up to eat. I think my stomach is rubbing up against my backbone, I'm so hungry."

Dobbs came in just as Turk was putting a sandwich at Dobb's place at the table. "You can start in on this and the coffee is almost ready," Turk said in a bit of a tired voice.

Soon Turk was placing a steamy cup of coffee down in front of Dobbs who muttered, "Hope I don't fall asleep in my supper."

It was not hard for the men to fall asleep and stay asleep until morning.

While unloading the wagons the next morning, a lot of talk passed between the old friends discussing all the news they had heard.

"I guess you could say that your friend May is going to be our neighbor," Dobbs joked.

"Maybe," Turk mused. "I just can't see her moving out of town and away from her boarding house."

While unloading supplies and still talking about the town news, the men were interrupted by Ryerson with a new friend stopping by.

"I want you to meet Sven Jensen," Ryerson spoke in a proud voice. "He moved here from Wisconsin a couple of months ago and he has a cabin up and almost ready for winter."

Turk and Dobbs shook the new-comers hand and said, "Welcome to Turk's trading post." We try to take care of your every need and wants."

"You can call me Sven," the slightly built settler said with a bit of an accent. "I got a wife and two strong boys and one little girl. We are so happy you have this old post here. We don't get to town much. Almost never."

"We come to trade," Ryerson declared as he put two jars of jam on the counter. "How much baking supplies can I get for these?"

Dobbs robbed his chin thoughtfully, "How about one big bag of flour?"

Ryerson dug out two more jars out of his bag. "One more of huckleberry and one of the best wild strawberry jam you ever ate. How about now?"

"Whoa, you got me with that wild strawberry jam," Dobbs didn't hesitate. "I think a bag of sugar, a bottle of vanilla and some baking soda."

"Throw in another bottle of vanilla and we have a deal," Ryerson countered.

"Done," Both men said together.

Sven strode over to the counter and fished two packages from his tote. ''Now this is the best tasting butter you could ever want, he boasted.

"I'll tell you something right off the bat," Turk said. "I have never had anyone trading butter yet and I wouldn't know how to judge a good trade. What are you looking for?"

"I need gloves for my two boys. They plumb wore their old ones out. Winter coming on, they need good gloves."

"We got them. Why don't we make it a pair for you too and as far as I'm concerned we have a trade." Dobbs smiled as he made the deal.

"Good deal," Sven was smiling also. "Do you have writing paper and pencils?"

"No, we have never stocked them," Dobbs answered him and then asked, "Do you need them?"

"My wife was teacher back in Wisconsin," Sven said proudly. "The wagon she drove here was full of books and maps and such. She is now teacher for our family and Ryerson's girls. They are running out of paper and the pencils are turning into little stubs."

"Hang on a minute," Dobbs offered as he took off for the lean-to and came back with some sheets of paper and a handful of pencils. "I won't be needing these this winter. You can put them to good use. Heaven knows, we can use all the educated people we can get in this part of the country, doncha think Turk?"

# Chapter Twelve

"I feel like we are eating like rich people," Dobbs declared as he slathered butter and jam on a hard-tack biscuit. "I swear I could spread this stuff on a block of wood and be happy eating it."

Neither man had special plans for the day. The supplies had all been put away. Dobbs had moved his cot into the post and settled in for the winter. The lean-to looked deserted and a little lonely. If they had needed extra room for the added supplies, it was available in the lean-to, but everything fitted neatly on the shelves in the post Dobbs had built shelves on all four walls and even in the two small bedrooms.

"Well, I'm not going to sit around all day," Dobbs spoke up. "I plan to gather some swamp grass and stack them in bundles. I might as well fill the lean-to with them. That way I'm pretty sure there will be enough food for the horses. They probably won't like it much, but it's better than going hungry."

Turk answered, "You are sure enough right about them not being crazy about swamp grass and also right about it would be better than going hungry. Almost anything is better than going hungry."

"If you are going to get busy, I guess I will too," Turk

declared as he got his sturdy body up from the chair by the stove. "I have been thinking along the same lines as you. I know we have a good wood supply, but a little more couldn't hurt."

Their chores kept the two men busy way past lunchtime. That was not unusual. Many days they worked right through lunch.

Dobbs got back to the post first and was relaxing and getting warm by the fire when Turk came through the door carrying a big canning jar.

"What are you planning on doing with that old jar, Turk?" Dobbs asked.

"I'm sort of using it in self defense," Turk answered. "I know Old Dog needs to stay here in the post with us, but he does smell like an old dog. I'm going to keep this jar filled with fresh pine branches."

Dobbs had to chuckle. "So what your saying is that you want this place to smell like a cross between smelly dog and a pine tree."

"Yes, that's what I'm saying. This trick I learned years ago from my dear mother. She always kept a canning jar on kitchen table. Sometimes filled with flowers, but lots of times with pine branches. I figure that's why the scent of pine reminds me of her. I have some real good memories of that old canning jar."

A thoughtful look passed over Turk's face and his clear gray eyes became soft and maybe just a bit misty.

Dobbs knew his old friend was remembering good times and he also knew that the bad times were best forgotten. Dobbs busied himself getting supper started.

"We might as well forget lunch again," Dobbs broke the silence. "Let's have an early supper." The supper ended up not being so early after all.

Both Turk and Dobbs jumped as they were startled by the bell over the door and surprised as Chief Crafty strode in.

"Hello Chief," Dobbs said with a welcoming grin. "What are you doing in these parts?"

"Want whiskey." The Indian did not mince words. "Trade baskets." He held up two cleverly woven baskets.

Turk wondered what Dobbs would do. You could get in a lot of trouble selling whiskey to the Indians. He didn't have to wonder long.

Dobbs disappeared into his bedroom and in a short while he came out with a pint jar not quite half full of whiskey.

"Sorry, Chief, this is all we have," Dobbs sounded like he really was sorry. "I'll give this to you. It isn't enough to bother trading for."

"Trade one basket." The Indian held up the smaller basket.

Dobbs didn't want to hurt Chief Crafty's pride so he reluctantly took the basket.

The Indian was not in a big hurry. They visited about the town gossip and about the railroad as it would come very close to his village. He talked about his people selling to the railroad workers. He had heard that the railroad paid their workers very good wages.

Finally he was ready to leave. As he opened the door, he turned around and announced, "Be back warm weather. Maybe then you have big bottle of whiskey."

Dobbs smiled at the Indian, "Probably not, friend. Big bottle of whiskey and old Indians just don't get along well together."

Turk and Dobbs could hear Chief Crafty laughing as he reached the trail leading down to the river.

"I'm sure glad he don't hold a grudge and is still our friend,"

Dobbs grinned as he said this.

"He is good natured and laid back, but I have the idea it is a whole lot better to have him as a friend and not an enemy."

Turk nodded his head in agreement. "I think that is true of a lot of settlers too. This is a hard land and a tough life. It makes men need a lot more friends and if possible a lot less enemies."

"Now how about that early supper?"

# Chapter Thirteen

It was the third week of December and bitter cold. It was warm and comfortable inside the trading post. So comfortable that Dobbs appeared to be napping, but he was not. Dobbs had his eyes closed, but his mind was very busy. Suddenly he jumped up and announced, "I have a great idea."

"I've been thinking it through and I'm going to do it," Dobbs was getting more excited as he spoke. "I am going to take some pairs of socks and some candy over to our neighbors. I'll just go to the Ryersons and let them share with the Jensens. I figure on how this winter, they will be our best customers, maybe our only ones, and this will be a good will gesture." Busily getting his tote bag down from its peg on the wall and quickly filling it, Dobb's laughed as he stated, "I feel a little like St. Nick."

Turk knew the weather was not good and he suspected a snowstorm may be brewing, but he also knew that when Dobb's set his mind on something, one way or another, it would be done.

After getting his horse saddled and bundling up in some extra clothes, Dobbs stood by the door and told Turk so long and let him know he would be back as soon as he was able.

"You know with all them clothes on you look a lot fatter," Turk joked. "I guess you could pass for that jolly old feller."

"Well as long as I stay jolly I guess that's the most important thing," Dobbs laughed going out the door. "I will be ho, ho, ho-ing on my way."

Neither man suspected that this day was going to turn serious and they would not be jolly for a considerable length of time.

Dobbs did have a pleasant ride and was at Ryersons homestead within the hour. His knock on the door was answered right away.

"Why Mr. Dobbs, what a nice surprise," Mrs. Ryerson greeted him. "I am so glad to see you. I had no idea how I was going to get that chair-pad you ordered over to you."

"That's part of the reason why I'm here." As he said this, he gave her a little wink. "The other part is I kind of wanted to see you."

Mrs. Ryerson was a wise woman and understood what Dobbs was trying to say without really saying anything.

"I want you girls to get some wood from the woodshed and stack it on the porch. Bundle up and get two armloads a piece." She was helping them into their outside clothes all the time she was talking.

The girls minded right away and didn't have one word to say. They always were well behaved and knew this is the way it should be.

As soon as the door closed behind them, Dobbs reached into his bag and brought out the socks and candy. "I figured one pair of socks each and one big bag of candy for your family and one for the Jensens. Maybe you would see that they get them before Christmas?" Dobbs asked.

"How generous of you and Mr. Turk." The woman's smile lit up her face. "Thank you so much and speaking of Mr. Turk, here is that chair-pad. I hope it meets with your approval."

"It's just perfect. How much do I owe you?" Dobbs asked politely.

"Not one single thing," Mrs. Ryerson answered. "After what you brought us today, I feel I should be paying you. Would you have a cup of coffee with us?"

"Thank you, but I think I better head back to the post," Dobbs turned to leave. "I think we are in for some kind of a storm and I want to beat it home."

Dobbs was right. A storm was moving in. After crossing the river, Dobbs gave the horse his head, figuring the horse had a better sense of direction. The going was getting tougher by the minute and Dobbs could only see a few feet in front of the struggling horse. That probably explains what happened next.

A terrified deer suddenly appeared in the trail. Something must have been chasing it and had been after it for a long time. The poor deer was so scared that it must have thought Dobbs was after it too. The deer lunged at the horse and as the horse sidestepped, Dobbs came tumbling out of the saddle and down a deep gully. The last thing he remembered was thinking with all these extra clothes on, it was not so bad. He didn't know about the sharp rock half-hidden in the new fallen snow. There was a very sharp sudden pain to the side of his head and then everything turned pitch black.

# Chapter Fourteen

Back at the post. Turk was keeping himself busy. He rearranged the shelf that held the socks. He swept the floor, actually twice. Finally he did something he rarely did, he started supper.

Dobbs had shot and cleaned a rabbit the day before. Turk washed it up good and browned it in an iron skillet. They cooked nearly all their meals in the same iron skillet Put in a little water after browning and you could let it cook as long as you wanted. Through all of his busy work, he could not shake an uneasy feeling. A feeling he had ever since Dobbs had left that morning.

"You are starting to act like a silly old mother hen," he told himself. "Dobbs is a grown man and can take care of himself with no help from you."

With nothing left to do and with all of his chores done, Turk sat down in a chair next to the woodstove. He looked over at Dobb's empty chair and gave a small sigh. The quiet and the warm fire combined to lull him into a deep sleep. When he awoke more than an hour later, he had not lost the uneasy feeling.

Getting to his feet and going to the window, he was not

surprised to see snowflakes coming down. "Maybe the snow has not started across the river yet." Turk mumbled to himself. "It is a ways from here. Maybe Dobbs decided not to risk the storm and to stay right where he was at the Ryersons." Turk was trying to find a good reason why Dobbs hadn't come home.

Time dragged on. Soon Turk found himself pacing the floor. Just when he decided he better do something, he heard a noise outside. Opening the door, he saw Dobb's horse standing by the railing. The tote bag was still hanging on the saddle ham, the rifle was still in its sling, the reins dragging on the ground, but no Dobbs.

Turk moved into action. Lighting a lantern, he led the horse to the barn. Checking the horse all over carefully, he was satisfied that nothing had happened to him. Taking off the saddle, he noticed the tote bag no longer held the sock and candy Dobbs had packed, but something Turk didn't recognize and had no time or inclination to check out.

His mind and heart were both racing. He saddled his own horse, knowing all along that something was very wrong.

Turk knew he would need to take along the lantern for light as by now the snowflakes were getting bigger and really coming down. The storm was getting serious. This was going to be one of those blizzards the old timers had warned him about. Turk started down the rugged path toward the river.

"I plumb can't see anything." Turk realized he was talking to his horse. "How will we ever find Dobbs in this snowstorm? He can't last long without freezing to death." This latest idea made Turk feel a little sick and gave him some added strength to press on.

"This is hopeless." Turk was getting desperate. "Lord help me." Turk found himself praying. He didn't know what else to do. "Dobbs is my best friend in all the world. He is a good man, a little ragged around the edges, but a good, good man."

"Dobbs! Dobbs!" Turk kept calling out in the darkness with all the power he could muster.

Miracle of miracles, he was sure he heard Old Dog's bark.

"Keep barking, you sweet old dog, keep on barking!" Turk called out into the storm. "Go to Old Dog," he urged his horse on. The barking got closer and Turk kept right on shouting.

Finally he reached the barking sound. Getting down off his mount and shining the lantern all about, he saw that lovely old dog and beside him the too still figure of Dobbs.

Hurrying down the gully to where they were in the snow, the first thing Turk noticed was the blood. Lots of blood. The snow all around them was dark with blood. Kneeling down by his old friend, he fearfully felt for a pulse on his neck, praying as he did so.

The pulse was so weak, he had to check again.

Dobbs face where it wasn't bloody was very pale. Turk had never seen Dobb's face so pale. Knowing that his unconscious friend would not last much longer out in the cold, Turk gathered him up and very gently put him belly down over the saddle.

Grabbing the reins in one hand and the lantern in the other, he ordered, "Old Dog, you take the lead. I know you have had a rough day and you have done so much already, but your sense of direction is better than mine. You know how to get back to the post and we both know we need to get our friend home."

# Chapter Fifteen

It was hard going along the rough snow-covered path, but Old Dog never wavered. The man and the animals kept up a steady pace. At last, Turk noticed the scent of wood smoke in the air.

"We have to be getting close," he said out loud. "I don't think anyone else in these parts have a fire."

There it was. Turk could barely see the post through the storm. Even harder to see was the faint light shining from the candle he had left burning.

As he gently lifted Dobbs from the saddle, he softly explained to the horse that he would have to wait to get back in the warmth of the barn. First he needed to get Dobbs inside and get him warm. Old Dog followed him inside.

Turk put his good friend on the floor as close as possible to the wood stove. He dragged Dobbs cot from the bedroom and throwing back the covers, he began removing the wet clothes from Dobbs half frozen still body.

He was soaked to the skin. Hard telling how long he had laid in the wet snow. The long ride home had the blood flowing again from the big gash on the side of Dobbs face.

"I'm giving you your Christmas gift early," Turk muttered

as he dressed Dobbs in the soft nightshirt he had ordered months ago from Josh. He recalled how Josh didn't think Dobbs would wear it and how Turk told him he would wear it if that was the case. I like wearing them nightshirts. It seems good to get out of that long underwear for a change.

After getting Dobbs in bed and covering him with the warmed up quilts. Turk rushed outside and took care of the patient horse. Both horses whinnied as if to greet each other. He made sure there was water in their tank and he threw extra hay into the manger.

The first thing he did when he got back inside was to put a pan of water on the stove to heat.

"I need to clean you up," Turk talked to Dobbs even though he knew he didn't hear him. "Let's see how bad you are hurt."

Dobbs never stirred as Turk cleaned the gaping wound, even when he dabbed some whisky on it. He wasn't sure if he was going the right thing, but it seemed right.

"If you were in town, I am sure the Doc would put some stitches in," he went on to say. He had checked for broken bones as he undressed him and didn't think there was any. Not even many bruises, probably because of the extra clothing. The head wound was bad he knew, but that seemed to be the worst of it.

Turk did not sleep at all that night. He gave Old Dog some fresh cold water and even a piece of the rabbit he had cooked earlier. Many times during the night, he checked on Dobbs and he never moved or made a sound. His pulse remained steady, but very weak.

As the sun came up, the storm raged on. It was getting colder and now the wind began to blow, swirling the snow and making it almost impossible to see anything.

Gradually there was a slight change in Dobbs breathing.

He moved slightly and made some moaning sounds. As Turk watched closely, Dobbs raised his hand to his head and tried to sit up. He looked around and in a weak voice asked, "Is this Heaven, did I make it, or am I still at that beautiful old trading post way out in the wilderness?"

# Chapter Sixteen

Hearing his master's voice, Old Dog jumped up from his comfortable beat-up rug in the corner and went to Dobbs wagging his tail with all his might. Dobbs reached down and rubbed the dog on his graying head.

''Old Dog saved your life and probably mine too," Turk told Dobbs. "He never left your side and kept you as warm as he could until I found you. I doubt we would have made our way home without him."

"He is a good old fellow," agreed Dobbs. "How is my horse? I sure hope he made it too."

"Don't worry, I've checked him twice," Turk explained. "I was waiting for you to come around before going to the barn and checking again. Do you remember what happened?"

Dobbs answered slowly, "The last thing I remember is a deer with a crazed look in her eyes lunging at the horse. I guess I wasn't expecting it and I plumb fell off. I can remember falling down a ravine and thinking this is not so bad. The next thing I know is a real sharp pain and that's all. The next thing I know is I am right here with the worst headache anyone has ever had.

It feels like someone is banging a sledge hammer against

the side of my head. I have figured out I can't make any quick moves without getting dizzy. Makes me more then a little sick to my stomach too."

Turk straightened Dobbs covers. "The best thing you can do is don't move." Concern was written all over Turk's handsome face. "I'm here and I'm not too busy," Turk told his old friend. "Whatever you want, just let me know. Now I'm talking within reason. How about starting with a little sip of water?"

"Well if you think that's reasonable, I'll give it a try," Dobb's voice was still weak, but a little bit of his old self was showing through.

He slept all the rest of the day. In the middle of the night, Turk heard him stirring. Getting up to light a candle, Turk asked him what he needed.

"I need to relieve myself," Dobbs said in a small voice. "I don't think I can make it to the outhouse."

"I already thought about that," Turk got a small bucket from under the bed. "You might not like it, but this will have to do until you are stronger."

Dobbs did grumble a bit, but he had little choice. Turk thought the grumbling was a good sing. Dobbs went right back to sleep until late the next morning.

When he awoke again, he was a little stronger. ''Do you think it would be reasonable to try to sit up a while?" Dobbs asked. "I don't think it would be reasonable to figure I'm going to stay in bed forever."

"You can try," Turk answered. "You won't know if you don't try."

When Dobbs slowly sat up in bed, his face turned chalky white and he started trembling. He clenched his teeth and forced himself to calm down.

"I'm as weak as a newborn colt," Dobbs muttered. "With about the same chance of standing without falling on down. How about trying about a half of a cup of your good coffee?"

''Now you are starting to sound like the Henry Dobbs I used to know," Turk joked. "You always said my coffee will either cure you or kill you!"

Dobbs did not sit up long. He soon found his head was better lying down flat on his back. He had no trouble falling sound asleep once more.

Turk had been soaking Dobb's bloody clothes ever since the accident. He guessed it was time to try to scrub them. It took a lot of scrubbing, but finally they were fairly clean, or at least as clean as he could get them. He draped the wet clothes over chairs and the counter. He knew the warm fire would dry them soon enough.

Knowing he had done all that needed to be done, Turk decided to make it an early night. After banking the fire in the woodstove and taking a final check on Dobbs, He went to bed. Before drifting off, it dawned on him that the next morning it would be Christmas Day. That would raise Dobb's spirits some.

Turk almost laughed out loud as he realized Dobbs had not even mentioned the nightshirt Turk had put on him. He thought it would be very interesting to hear what Dobbs reaction may be.

# Chapter Seventeen

It didn't take long to find out Dobb's reaction.

Turk had got up and took special care in dressing for the day. All clean clothes including long underwear and socks. His thinking was that if you didn't dress up for Christmas, then when would you?

Coming out of his bedroom, he was surprised to see Dobbs awake and sitting on his cot. His mean-looking wound made him look a bit fierce as he said, "Doncha think it's really sad when a feller is down and out and can't really defend himself and his good friend puts a dress on him? I'm surprised you didn't curl my hair and put rouge on me while you were at it."

Turk tried to be serious. "You know that's not a dress, it's a nightshirt. When I put it on you, I wasn't sure what kind of shape you were in and I needed to get you warmed up as soon as possible. For your information I ordered that nightshirt for you from Josh at the general store. I like mine so well, I was hoping you might like one too. I guess you could say it was to be your gift for Christmas."

''Well thanks, I guess. As a matter of fact, it will work out just fine for now. You might as well know, I'll be looking forward to getting into my scratchy old long underwear when

I'm all well. I don't think I am a nightshirt kind of man."

"I hate to admit it, but Josh was right on the money," Turk explained. "He said you wouldn't wear it. I can't hardly wait to tell him, he was right. He enjoys being right so much. By the way, Merry Christmas."

Dobbs broke out in the first smile he had on his face since the accident. "You mean today is Christmas? Well, Merry Christmas to you too."

When Turk went out to take care of the horses and the chickens, he found the storm had passed and left beautiful snowy white drifts all around the trading post. Before going back inside, he gathered an armful of cedar boughs to replace the old ones in the canning jar on the table. He figured they would add a festive look to the place and make it smell better at the same time.

As he opened the door, Dobbs was standing just inside.

"Don't take your jacket off," Dobbs ordered. "Go back out to the barn and in the northeast corner of the lean-to under a pile of hay is your present. Then look inside my tote bag and you will find the rest of it. I'm going to stand here in the doorway for a little while and get some fresh air."

Turk found the well made rocker and the chair pad that fit it and was so pleased. "This has got to be the best rocker in the whole wide world," he declared. "Now I really feel bad about that silly old nightshirt."

''No don't you dare even think that." Dobbs spoke with a sureness in his voice. "After all between you and Old Dog you saved my life. If you hadn't went out in the storm looking for me, I probably wouldn't be sitting here in this cute little outfit."

The two old friends had an especially nice breakfast. Eggs and biscuits with lots of wild strawberry jam and lots of butter.

Followed by many cups of Dobbs good hot coffee.

Turk moved his old chair into his bedroom and put his new rocker close to the stove. Dobbs sat down in his chair on the other side of the stove. Both men seemed to be lost in their own thoughts. Dobbs thinking what a lucky man he was to have survived. He was glad to be feeling better and even more glad to have a faithful friend like Turk His friend Turk was lost in Christmas memories of his days on the farm with his mother.

After more than a few moments of silence, Dobbs spoke. "I guess I better think about starting to celebrate my birthday."

"Whoa, is today your birthday?" Turk wanted to know.

"I plain just don't know for sure," Dobbs answered. "No one seems to know for sure. I asked my Pa and he said I was born in the winter, but he didn't recollect which day. I always celebrated on Christmas Day because I figured if it was good enough for the baby Jesus and it would be plenty good enough for me."

Turk had an idea. "Do you feel up to a real drink, Dobbs?"

"I'm willing to try," Dobbs smiled as he answered. "You know, I have been smelling whiskey ever since I got up and around. Did you give me some whiskey to help bring me around?"

"No but I did pour some on that cut to clean it out and I might have spilled some on your pretty new nightshirt," Turk said. "If I did, I am sure sorry."

Their first drink was to toast Dobbs' Birthday. The second drink was to wish each other Merry Christmas. Many drinks later, they found themselves toasting Old Dog.

Sometime that jolly afternoon they started laughing about their situation.

Dobbs was laughing as he said, "I sure hope no one happens

by and fins us two old half-drunk men. One sitting in a fancy new rocker and the other with a gash on his face sitting here in a fancy new dress!"

Both men were ready to go to bed rather early Christmas night. Before going to bed, they went out and lingered a bit on the porch. The full bright moon cast a perfect light over the small lake and the trees surrounding the post. The scene was so perfect that there was really nothing to say.

"I know it is most unusual, but I can't think of a solitary thing to add to this day," Dobbs said in a solemn voice.

Turk agreed.

# Chapter Eighteen

Dobbs was happy. A day and a half later, he was able to get into his long underwear. He made a big deal out of it. "Out of all my worldly possessions, the one I am most happy to bequeath to you is this silly outfit," he told Turk. "May you wear it in good health all your days."

The cut on his face was starting to heal. It looked like the scar would be from the middle of his cheek almost to his chin. If it had been closer to his hair line, he could have covered it some with his hair. "So, would you say you are a lot better?"

Without waiting for an answer, Turk went on to say that he was afraid that Dobbs needed to do something about all the matted dried blood still in his hair. "The reasonable thing to do would be to take a nice long warm bath."

"I guess you are right," Dobbs agreed. "I know I have caked on blood in one ear too. This is about my least favorite thing to do, you know. I will have to be careful not to get that cut bleeding again. You do come up with some great ideas, old buddy of mine."

"If you like that idea, you are going to love my next one. When you get done with your bath, I'm going to get Old Dog in the tub and wash your dried blood out of his hair too." Turk was smiling all time he was saying this.

Across the room, Old Dog's ears perked up as he heard his name. He wagged his tail back and forth across the wood floor. Usually when they mentioned his name it meant something good. Like a ride or a treat.

"You know, Turk, You do have a bit of a mean streak in you. You act like you are really enjoying this. You are, aren't you?" Dobbs asked.

"You better believe it" Turk answered with a big grin. "This is the most fun I've had since Christmas. I'm going to do the outdoor chores and give you some privacy. Our woodpile is down quite a lot since that big storm, so I need to get a lot of wood from the shed. I've already heated a few buckets of water and you do remember where we keep the soap. Take your time and enjoy your nice sudsy warm bath.

Dobbs could still hear Turk laughing as he closed the door and went across the porch.

About an hour later, Turk was done with his work and came back inside. Dobbs was dressed and sitting near the stove. Turk looked at him and commented, "You look real shiny and clean. I see you didn't start up the bleeding again. Good work!"

Taking off his jacket, he went over to the sleeping dog. "It's your turn now, old feller."

It wasn't long before he realized that getting Old Dog into the tub was going to be a lot less fun. It was pretty obvious the dog was not going to willingly take a bath. Turk picked him up and more or less wrestled him into the water, but not for long. Old Dog jumped out and Turk knew he was going to have to hold him down with one hand and soap him up with the other. What he forgot was that soap was going to make it a lot harder to keep a grasp on the strong dog. Soon the soapy dog was running around in circles with Turk right behind him. Turk backed him into a corner and picked him up one more time and dunked him clear under the water. He bodily picked him up and dunked him clear under again. Taking him out and trying to dry him, Turk declared, "This will have to do." It was hard to tell who had got the wettest.

Dobbs was laughing so hard, it was actually hurting his face. "Oh please, stop. You are making me hurt. Don't get me bleeding again." He had tears rolling down his face and the salty tears hurt too.

Turk flopped down in his rocker. "I'm soaked and tired and I will never give that dog another bath. From now on you can both just stay dirty as far as I'm concerned."

This started Dobbs off on another round of laughter. "Sure am happy to hear that and I'll bet Old Dog is happy too."

# Chapter Nineteen

The snow never went completely away and the river did freeze over. Dobbs and Turk were not sure how thick the ice was, but it was strong enough for a horse to cross over on it.

About once a week, either Jensen or Ryerson came over for supplies. They knew the river ice over the shallow part was plenty strong enough for their horses. Sometimes they came together and the four men would have a good long visit.

Most of the talk was about each of their Spring plans. They talked of planting different crops and clearing some more of their land. Ryerson and Jensen had made a good deal. Ryerson had put his work on hold to help Jensen get his cabin up before bad weather. In return, Jensen's two strong sons would come over to Ryerson's every other day to help him get his crops in.

Ryerson laughed as he joked, "I love my three little girls. I wouldn't give them up for nothing, but they can't help me much on the farm. They do work in our little vegetable garden and they are a great help to their mother."

"Yeah, I was pretty smart having them two boys," Jensen joked right back. "Maybe I think you did not think that having kids thing through good enough."

Dobbs spoke up, "When we start discussing kids, old Turk

and me can't say much, but do you see that smart looking dog laying over there in the corner? You might think he is asleep, but he's listening. I believe he's about the smartest dog around these parts. What do you think, Turk?"

"Well, I don't know about smart, but I'll bet he's about the strongest one around." He had given Dobbs a perfect opening to talk about that infamous bath, but Dobbs didn't say a word. He didn't even look like he wanted to say anything.

The four men enjoyed their visits together. No others came to the trading post that first winter, so the two partners were very glad to see the two neighbors. They would mostly bring baked goods to trade.

Shortly after Dobbs accident, Ryerson had a special jar of wild strawberry jam that he handed to Dobbs. The Mrs. said I am not trading this jam. I should just make it a gift for you. She feels bad because you had been bringing those gifts to us when you got hurt."

"She knows my weakness," Dobbs said. "I would never turn down a jar of this jam. It's by far the best I ever had."

"I agree." Ryerson answered. "It was so lucky the girls found that strawberry patch. They check it all the time waiting for the berries to ripen. They worry that bears might beat them to it. Do you think there are bears around here?"

"Yes, I do," Dobbs offered his opinion. "I sometimes worry about Old Dog wandering and sniffing around. I sure hope be never runs into one."

Turk broke into the conversation. "Well if he ever does, I feel sorry for the poor old bear." Still not a word from Dobbs. He was going to wait and pick the perfect time to tell about Turk's tussle with the dog.

As Dobbs filled the men's totes with supplies, he always managed to slip a few pieces of hard candy into them as a surprise.

At last, Spring came to Turk's trading post. The snow slowly melted. The ice on Lake Henry gave away first and then the river ice followed. You could hear birds singing in the early morning and hoot owls making noise late at night.

The land around the post was very wet, just as the men expected it to be. They figured the swampy ground would take a while to dry. Each day the warm sun helped and the Spring breezes did their part too.

"I'm not going to be in a hurry to go to Muskie City," Turk was telling Dobbs as they were having their morning coffee on the porch. "I don't want to get stuck in the mud half-way there. That wouldn't be a fun way to spend the day."

"Give it another couple of weeks." Dobbs suggested. "We are running low on some things, but we still have plenty of beans."

Turk smiled at his friend. "That sure takes some worry off my mind. We won't be running short on hay or wood either. I guess we figured about right."

The days were lazy days. Not much to do this time of year, but both men knew the time would soon come when their days would be busy again.

Finally one evening, Turk announced he would be getting up very early the next morning and heading into town. He had a long list of supplies and had no idea that this trip into Muskie City would change his life forever.

# Chapter Twenty

The mid-morning sun shone down on the roofs of Muskie City. Stopping on the rise outside of town, Turk observed how busy the streets were, people rushing here and there. Even here on the hill, he could see how men had been working. He drove over to better read a hand-painted sign on the river bank. It read: "Coming soon Mayville Park."

"Very nice," Turk said out loud. May had told him she was going to have a park built for the town. He could even see the start of the covered dock she also said she was going to make happen. A woman of many talents, he decided as he drove down into town.

Stopping in front of the general store, he was just in time to catch the sight of Jessie all dressed up, and heading somewhere.

"Oh Turk, Jessie gushed as she gave him a big hug. "I'm so happy to see you. Please stick around a while. I'll be back in a jiffy and we can have a nice visit. We have a lot to talk about."

Going inside, Turk greeted Josh who was standing as always, behind the counter by the cash drawer.

"Howdy, Josh," Turk hailed the store owner in a hearty voice. "Where is Jessie off to in such a hurry?"

"Good to see you," Josh smiled at Turk. "You know Jessie, she has a new project and she is all excited about it. A new preacher came to town and he has the women all fired up. They formed a group called the Muskie City Christian Ladies Aid Society. Everyone of those ladies are doing their best at trying to please that new preacher. Believe or not, Jessie is the president, May is the treasurer and a new woman in town is the secretary. I think you know her. She is Mrs. Elizabeth Evans."

"No, that don't ring a bell," Turk answered. "I don't recall that name."

"Did you have a good winter? Is Dobbs doing okay? Did you have enough supplies?" Josh was firing questions quicker than Turk could answer them.

"Yes, yes and yes," Turk finally got a word in. "I do have a long list today though. What's new around here?"

"Well, I guess we got too excited about that railroad. It will happen, but not for a few years. They are laying tracks and a bridge over a river south of here and they have to build a bridge over our river too. I figure it takes quite a while to build a railroad bridge."

Turk leaned his lanky body against the counter. "I noticed some work being done on May's park up on the hill."

"Yep," Josh smiled as he said, "That woman is something else. Her boarding house is going great guns. It has become the place to go and eat. Jessie and me go there a few times a week ourselves."

Turk thought for a moment, "Maybe I'll saunter over there myself and try it out. While I'm at it, I might check out the town and see what's new.

There was a twinkle in Josh's eye as he said, "You do that, Turk. You never know what you might find. You might even

76

be pleasantly surprised. You take some time, this is a good sized list. No need to hurry."

Driving the horse and wagon to the livery stable, Turk did see some new buildings, but he didn't take time to check them over. His horse was probably hungry and more than a little thirsty. Leaving the livery and walking down the boardwalk, one of the new buildings did catch his eye.

The sign over the big window in front said, "Canning Jar Clothiers." In the middle of the window was an old canning jar filled with what he guessed was silk flowers.

"How strange," Turk thought to himself. He had never figured there might be someone besides himself that was fond of flowers in jars.

It was almost like he was somehow drawn to the door. It took a few seconds to get his eyes adjusted after coming in from the bright sunshine. As he stood there, he could see someone sitting at some kind of a contraption working away. He knew it was a woman. The sun coming through the window made the back of her pinned up hair shine like burnished gold.

Turk cleared his throat and in a firm voice said, "Good Day. I thought I would stop in and see what kind of a shop you have here."

The woman got up and came over to Turk. Her hair really was the color of burnished gold and it framed the sweetest face that he had ever seen. Her eyes were a beautiful soft green, just like the lake back at the post will get in a certain light. She was a tiny little thing, but it was easy to see she was all woman.

"Hello there, Mr. John Turk. I knew someday you would walk into my shop and I'm so happy to see you. You don't remember me, do you?" She held out her small hand.

Turk didn't answer. He took her hand, but he didn't answer.

"I'm Hester Lee Evans from back home," she told him with an extra sweet smile. That smile was the final thing that added to Turks confusion.

After more than a few seconds, Turk finally found his voice. "But, you were just a little girl. I remember you hanging around Dobbs store and listening to his tall stories."

"That was me, John." Hester Lee told him in a voice that he thought sounded sweeter every time he heard it As he stood there still holding her hand, she placed her other hand over his, "I guess I grew up as little girls will and I became a young woman."

Turk shakily added, "Yes, Mam, I guess you sure did that alright enough"

Something very strange had happened. He thought he could stand and hold this beautiful woman's hand forever, but it was not to be.

The door swung open and a young man came strolling in. "Sorry I'm a little late for our lunch date, Hester Lee. I've been thinking about this all morning. Are you ready to go?"

# Chapter Twenty-One

"Hello Billy," Hester Lee said as she took her hand away from Turk's hand reluctantly. "I can be ready in a jiffy. I'd like to have you meet an old friend of mine, John Turk, who has the trading post outside of town. John, this is Billy Scutter."

The two men sized each other up as they shook hands. Turk was trying to find fault with Billy, but he could not. He was a clean-cut friendly young man and in spite of himself he liked what he saw.

"Would you like to join us?" Billy asked politely. "We are going down the street to Mays."

"No thank you," John answered back. "I only came to town for supplies and I have a long ride ahead of me back to the post." His plans of having another taste of May's fine cooking had completely slipped his mind.

Hester Lee paused in the doorway as she was leaving. "John, will you please stop in before you leave? Aunt Elizabeth will be so disappointed if she doesn't get to see you. She will be here soon. We never leave the shop unattended for long."

Turk opened his mouth to say no, he wouldn't have the time, but looking down into those soft green eyes and seeing the little smile playing on her sweet lips, he found himself saying, "Yes, of course. I have time for Aunt Elizabeth. After I get the supplies loaded, I I will be back for a quick visit."

Getting the horse and wagon from the livery and helping Josh load the supplies, he felt strangely like somehow his whole world had changed.

Josh noticed that Turk was not very talkative and his mind seemed to be somewhere else. He did ask if Dobbs was going to be coming into town anytime soon.

"You can bet on it," Turk answered Josh. "He has a new story and I'm sure he is anxious to tell you all about it." He didn't add that he was also sure he would want to come and see Hester Lee.

Turk arrived back at the clothing store at the same time as Aunt Elizabeth.

"Hello, Mrs. Evans." Turk took her offered hand. "It's been a long time and I am so surprised to see you here in Muskie City."

He didn't remember her very well, but seeing her kind of jogged his memory. She had not changed a lot. Still wore her gray hair in a neat tight bun. Still had her glasses perched low on her nose and still dressed all in gray. Elizabeth Evans was as prim and proper as they come and Turk had an idea her clear gray eyes peering through them glasses didn't miss much.

"Hello there yourself, Mr. Turk," She shook his hand with some authority. "Have you had a chance to see Hester Lee? She was saying every day that she hoped you would come to town soon."

Before he could say anything, Hester Lee came hurrying in, explaining how happy she was to see him again.

Turk's visit ended up not being a quick visit. The time just flew by as they talked about the old days back home. The two ladies insisted on making some tea and they made sure that

Turk ate a very big piece of cake to go with it.

"Do you like the tea, John?" Hester Lee asked him in that voice that pleased Turk so much.

"It is very good," Turk assured her even though he had never tasted tea before. "This cake is about the best I've ever had." He didn't know if that was because he was so hungry or if it was because he was sitting here next to this beautiful woman. He really didn't want to leave, but realized he needed to make a move.

"I have to head back to the post now. It is a long trip and I won't be getting back before dark. But that's alright, I have went back in the dark before."

"Oh I feel it is my fault. I shouldn't have asked you to stay so long. I'm sorry, it's just that we had so much to talk about. Please be careful on the trail, John. I would feel terrible if something was to happen to you."

Hester Lee was holding Turk's hand again and Turk had the feeling that if he didn't leave right now, he may never be able to leave at all.

# Chapter Twenty-Two

Turk did not travel home in the dark after all. It was one of those early Spring nights when the moon seemed to shine brighter than usual. The moonlight made the trail easier to follow.

May's recently bought property had more than a trail. It was more like a well-traveled road. She had hired loggers to cut trees and skid them to the river. Using the same road for skidding the logs had made the road much better. Turk thought maybe he and Dobbs should consider loggers to cut some trees. It would sure be nice to go all the way into town on a good road.

All the way home from Muskie City, his mind was full of thoughts of Hester Lee. Turk, who was usually so confident, was confused. This was a new feeling for him and he wasn't even sure how he felt about it.

Pulling up to the dimly lit post, Turk was not surprised to see Dobbs come rushing out to help in unloading the wagon.

"Did you buy Josh plumb out?" he inquired.

"No," Turk answered. "I got just what was on the list. No more, no less."

After they had taken the supplies inside, Dobbs suggested

he would take care of the horse and wagon if Turk wanted to have his supper while it was still warm. Turk was not particularly hungry, but he was never one to pass up a good deal. So he agreed.

When Dobbs came in from the barn, he was full of questions. "Is there anything new going on in town?" he asked as he made himself comfortable at the table.

"Sure is," Turk said. "Let's see. May is having her Park built and having trees cut on her property. You will be pleased when you see the road the loggers made. Also there is a new shop in town. It's a clothing store. A very nice clothing store."

"Must be giving Josh and Jessie a little competition," Dobbs commented. "You didn't happen to stop at the post office to see if a letter had come from Hester Lee, did you?"

"No," Turk answered with a grin. "I figure if she wanted you to have a letter, she would have given it to me."

"Are you telling me that Hester Lee is in Muskie City?" Dobbs was scratching his head a little as he said this. "Is it her clothing store?"

"Yep, she is there alright enough. I couldn't believe my eyes. Her Aunt Elizabeth is with her and I guess business is booming. They both seem pretty contented and happy to be here. They wanted to know if you would be coming into town soon. I told them I was sure you would be."

Dobbs had already made up his mind. "You can be sure I will. This is a nice surprise. I suppose she has changed some after all these years."

"I guess you could say that," Turk agreed. "She sure doesn't look like the skinny freckle-faced kid that hung around your old store all the time. I used to wonder if she couldn't find something better to do. I recall that her folks died and left her in the care of her aunt and uncle. Something must have happened to him, because I don't think he is with them."

During this conversation, Dobbs noticed there was a different look on Turk's face. His face looked softer and even somewhat dazed. This was strange, not at all like Turk.

"I think I will go to town someday next week," Dobbs announced. "I haven't had a decent hair cut or shave since last Fall, not even a bath since that one you made me take at Christmastime. Believe it or not, I will even take a bath before I go. I want to look good for Hester Lee and her aunt."

"You will probably stay here and keep an eye on things, won't you?" Dobbs asked trying to keep a serious look on his face.

"Maybe," Turk answered. "I'm not sure. Maybe I'll just ride along and get a hair cut and shave too. I sure don't like the notion that you might be better looking than me. I don't think I could live with that."

The days seemed to drag on slowly. Finally Turk could stand it no longer.

"Why do we have to wait until next week? I don't see why we can't get up early tomorrow morning and close the post for the day and go to town."

The two men talked it over and decided it was a fine idea. They both went to bed early, but Turk had trouble falling asleep. After more than a few restless hours, he got up and dressed and started hitching up one of the horses. They figured they would go together and pick up some extra supplies or maybe they wouldn't even get anything. It just didn't seem right to go to town and not pick up something.

Dobbs had slept very well after taking his warm bath. He was surprised when he awoke to find Turk gone. Going to the door in his long underwear, he saw Turk pacing back and forth alongside the wagon.

"You are sure in a big hurry today," Dobbs mentioned. "Can you at least wait until I get dressed and have a cup of coffee? I am willing to get along without breakfast, but I don't think the town is ready to see me in my birthday suit. And you wouldn't enjoy me as a companion for the trip if you don't let me have my coffee."

Turk was impatient, "Well, if a body is going somewhere, I don't see any reason to waste time."

Dobbs took that to mean he would not be getting any breakfast. He knew something was going on with his old friend and he was starting to guess what it was.

# Chapter Twenty-Three

The two old friends enjoyed their trip into Muskie City. The closer they came to town, the less agitated Turk was. They talked a lot, but even the quiet moments between them were comfortable.

Stopping on the rise at the edge of town, it was easy to see that Mayville Park was coming right along. The pavilion close to the bank of the river was nearly finished. The playground area was filling up with swings and picnic tables. Scattered around under the trees were many benches. The two men agreed that it was going to be quite a nice park.

Driving down the hill, they went straight to the barber shop.

"You go ahead first," Dobbs generously offered. "I will see to the horse and wagon. It will take a while to get you looking good, so I will wait for you at the general store. Come and let me know when it is my turn. It won't take long for me. If you don't want to wait for me, just tell the girls I'll be along soon."

''No, I'll wait until we can go together." Turk said. "We can visit a while then maybe you will be ready for something to eat."

Dobbs gave a little grin as he nodded his head in agreement, "You do have the best ideas, Turk."

Driving the wagon into the livery stable and jumping down, Dobbs handed the reins to the old man who took care of the place.

"Hey, isn't this Turk's horse?" he asked.

"Sure is," Dobbs answered. "You have a good eye for horses. I'm Turk's partner Dobbs." Shaking his hand he explained about not coming to town often. "I prefer staying out at the post."

"Nice to meet you," the old man said as he looked closely at Dobbs. "Where did you get that mean looking scar?"

Dobbs had been waiting for this question. He tried to look serious and said one word. "Indian."

The old man's eyes became big and he exclaimed, "What happened?"

"The only thing more I'm going to say, is, You will take notice that my scalp is intact and I still have all my hair."

When both men were ready, they did go to visit Hester Lee and her aunt. There were so happy to se the two men. There were lots of hugs and smiles all around.

"What a nice surprise," Hester Lee said in her soft sweet voice. "I didn't dare hope you would both be here so soon."

Aunt Elizabeth spoke up, "I wish we could offer you some food, but all we have is tea and coffee."

"I vote we all go to May's for a late breakfast," Dobbs suggested. Everyone quickly agreed.

Closing the shop door behind her, it seemed natural for Hester Lee to take Turk's arm.

''Is it alright with you if i take your arm, John?" Turk didn't answer, but his expression said it for him.

May's boarding house was close by. Because it was a little late for breakfast and too early for lunch, the place was nearly empty. Stepping inside, Turk saw the clever Indian basket he had given May last summer. She was using it as an umbrella stand and there were two frilly umbrellas standing upright that you knew for sure belonged to May.

May came out of the kitchen and greeted them warmly. There were more hugs for the two men. "Johnny, you devil, you have got more handsome since last Fall." She gushed. "Dobbs you couldn't get any handsomer. Oh my, what have you done to your face?"

"I will give you the short version," Dobbs explained. "I plumb fell off my horse and landed on about the sharpest rock there ever was. Now the long version is a lot more interesting. Let me know when you are ready for that. Jessie and Josh heard one of my long versions and I'm sure you will hear it from them soon."

"I'm sure of that too, Dobbs. Now what can I get for you good people?"

"Breakfast," Dobbs stated. "I'm good and hungry. Turk wouldn't let me eat before we left home, and coffee, lots of coffee."

"Just toast for me," Aunt Elizabeth spoke up.

"And me," Hester Lee added.

May looked at Turk. Pushing back a few curls with one hand and the other on her hip, with a wink she asked, "What can I do for you, Johnny?"

"I will go with breakfast too, May," Turk answered.

They were still talking and drinking coffee when the lunch crowd started coming in, but May did not hurry them. She kept refilling their cups and joking with them in between her kitchen chores. When Turk took care of the bill, he made sure there was a very generous tip included.

As they were leaving. May couldn't help herself. "If you get hungry again before you go back to the post, remember I do serve the best chicken and dumplings in town"

Walking on the boardwalk back to the shop, Hester Lee glanced at Turk and asked, "Are you alright, John? You look a little flushed."

"I am fine," Turk smiled down at Hester Lee. "Actually I might be better than fine. I can't remember a day any more fine than this one."

The rest of the day flew by. Dobbs finally spoke up, "Turk, old buddy, we need to be getting on home. Old Dog has been taking care of the place I'm sure, but he probably needs a break."

Before they left, May came bustling in on a cloud of perfume and powder.

"I'm glad I caught you boys," she gushed on in her flirty May voice. "In two weeks we are having the grand opening of my park. There will be games and prizes and tons of good food. I want you both to come. Please say yes."

"Of course we will be there," Dobbs spoke for both of them. "Wouldn't miss it for anything."

The two men finally had to leave. As they were leaving, both waved and Turk yelled back, "We will see you soon," already thinking that two weeks seemed like a long time.

# Chapter Twenty-Four

The next week at the post was busy. A few loggers stopped in for supplies. There were more loggers arriving daily. The news was out about the stands of white pine and the many tall maple trees. So many of the trees needed to be cut because they had reached maturity and would start to decay and soon become dead trees that would not be suitable for lumber. The trees would only be good for firewood. Most of the loggers were too busy to stay and have a cup of coffee, but it was always offered.

Dobbs had started tilling the ground and already had planted early potatoes. The potatoes from last summer's crop were getting sparse, so Dobbs was hoping there would be an early summer. He was using the last of tile cabbage and parsnips. The root cellar had kept the vegetables well.

One particularly sunny day, Turk tore both beds apart and washed the blankets. After scrubbing them as good as he could, he draped them over the porch railing. The warm breeze and the sunshine dried them in one day, which was good. He didn't want to explain to Dobbs why there were no covers on his bed. While they dried, he mopped the floor and washed the only two windows they had. Looking around he decided if Old Dog wanted his rug washed he could drag it outside some rainy day and do it himself. He knew for sure he was not going to wash it.

After supper while on the porch sipping their coffee was the only time the men really had a chance to talk.

One evening Turk asked if Dobbs would till him in on the story he had told Jessie and Josh about his accident.

"Sure, it's a lot better than what really happened." Dobbs took another sip before he started. "I told them I was minding my own business, cutting some wood when this big old black bear got curious. He came too close, so I shot him, but I made the mistake of not making sure he was dead. That nosy old bear had just enough left in him to reach up and snag me a good one across my cheek, but I had the last word. I now have the softest bearskin rug on my bedroom floor. Every morning when I jump out of bed and feel that nice warm soft fur, I have to thank that bear all over again."

When Turk finished laughing, he said, "That is a better story. Did you make up something to tell the barber too?"

"Just a little bit of one," Dobbs answered. "The only made-up part was, it was a mean pack of hungry wolves that spooked my horse and after I got bucked off, I spent two days trying to find the post again. For a while, I couldn't remember who I was or where I lived. Someday I will tell everyone the true story, but not now. I'm having way too much fun."

The next day was Sunday and the two men spent the early morning trying to decide which chores they were going to do. After Dobbs put together a venison stew and had it on the stove starting to cook, they hadn't come to a decision which turned out to be a good thing. Suddenly they could hear someone coming down the trail. Coming into sight, they were delighted to see it was Josh driving one of the fancy buggies from the livery stable with Jessie sitting next to him. In the back seat in all her glory holding a fancy umbrella over her bleached curls was May. Next to her was Hester Lee. Turk's heart nearly jumped right out of his chest. He rushed over to the buggy and reached up to help her down. The green dress she was wearing had little dots of white and she was wearing the greatest white hat with green ribbons. The green from her dress made her eyes more greener than ever. Turk was sure he had never seen a more beautiful woman.

It was noisy bunch and everyone was talking at once.

Hester Lee explaining how her Aunt Elizabeth wanted to come, but she had a rush order for a lady who thought she needed a dress right away. Josh and Jessie were saying they were anxious to see any changes made at the post May gushing about how her coming was a last minute decision when she found out there would be room for her. May had never been to the trading post and was more than a little curious.

What a great day it turned out to be. Dobbs added to the venison stew he had put on earlier and it was done to perfection after everyone had looked the post over carefully.

"Your place is even nicer than I imagined it to be," Hester Lee told Turk. "You should be very proud of yourself, John."

Turk guessed he must be grinning like a fool, but he couldn't help it.

While still at the table eating, Josh asked, "Dobbs, do you suppose I could have a look at that bearskin rug?"

There was a little silence before Dobbs answered, "I wish I could show it to you, but I guess I didn't cure the skin good enough and the thing got so smelly, I had to get ride of it."

"I'm disappointed," Josh said with a big smile on his face. "I sure had my heart set on seeing that famous bearskin rug.

Actually that was the real reason for this trip."

The rest of the day was spent walking around the lake and enjoying the warm breezes together. There was so much to see that none of them realized the sun was starting to go down.

"Sorry, ladies, it's time to go," Josh announced. "Let's load up and head out."

May gave Turk and Dobbs a big hug and reminded them of the next Sunday and the dedication of the park. Hester Lee looked a little sad as she said, "I really hate leaving, but Sunday will be here before we know it."

Turk had the same look on his face. "Thank you all so much for coming to see our trading post. I'm glad you liked it. It means more to me than I can say. See you next Sunday."

He didn't add that he figured he would be seeing her in his dreams all week.

# Chapter Twenty-Five

Although Dobbs and Turk made it to the park before noon, the celebration was well on its way. The men took care of the horse before joining in. Dobbs took the bucket he had brought along down to the river so there would be cool water for the horse to drink. Turk rubbed the horse down with a chore cloth he had stored in the wagon, because he knew horses liked a familiar smell when they were around strange horses. They liked it even better if the cloth smelled like horse manure.

"Sure is a good turnout, doncha think Turk?" Dobbs asked.

Turk answered right away. "I think everyone in town thinks a lot of May and are very grateful for this good park."

Spying the table where Hester Lee sat was easy. There were four young men gathered around her. Turk recognized Billy Scutter, but he didn't know the others.

"Come sit with me, John," Hester Lee shouted as she caught sight of the men. "You too, Mr. Dobbs."

Hester Lee looked so pretty, it wasn't hard to see why she drew so much attention. Her reddish-gold bouncy curls were piled on top of her head with a fancy hair clip. Turk knew it was just a matter of time until some of the strands would come loose and frame her face. He also knew that he wanted to touch the strands and see if they were as soft as he figured they might be. Her dress was white with a yellow design running through it. She had on a matching bonnet that was fetchingly hanging down her back by the yellow strings. She knew the shade tree would keep the sun off her face for now, but later she would need to put her bonnet on.

Dobbs told Hester Lee, "Thanks for the invite, but I guess I will wander around and see who I can find."

Turk didn't hesitate. He was happy to sit at the table. The only way he could be happier is if the other men decided to move on.

The park was getting to be a noisy place. There was a fiddler playing some songs. Some people were trying to sing along. The children's shouts from the playground could be heard above everything else. The new swings were kept particularly busy.

The food table was loaded with all kinds of good food from the settler's kitchens. It was almost like they had tried to out-do each other. People just wandered in and filled their plates and then found a bench or a table. There was jugs of sweet tea on nearly every table, but the table that was the busiest was the beer table.

In the midst of all the noise, Mr. Scutter was the first to make a short speech.

"Settle down now," he informed the crowd. "It's time for the dedication. First I'm going to ask the good Reverend to say a little prayer." The prayer went on a little long. The preacher knew there were many folks here he had never seen in church. As long as he had their attention, he ought to give them a little talking to. At last he got around to talking about May and the great park she had given the town. He concluded with saying, "Let's put our hands together for Miss May Stone, about the best thing to ever happen to Muskie City."

After the whoops and whistles died down, May made her way to the platform inside the pavilion, "I don't know who this Miss May Stone person is, but she sounds like a hell of a woman." More shouts and whistles followed. "You all know me as just plain May. Now May could be called many things, but certainly never just plain." The crowd realized this and the hollering and noise started all over again. "I want to add a big thank you to each and every one for coming to Mayville Park today and making this the happiest day of my life so far. I say so far because I am just getting started. I have some great plans for Muskie City. Shucks, I've got some ides that scare even me. Now eat some more and drink some more and have the best time you can have." That really set the crowd off, but they proceeded to do just that.

The rest of the day passed quickly. There were three-legged races and horse shoe games and dancing amid more eating and drinking.

Turk would have been content to sit and talk to Hester Lee forever, but soon the sun was going down and there was a little chill in the air. The celebration was getting rowdy and most of the families had left. The noisiest of the men were walking down the hill and heading for the saloons in town.

Turk turned to Hester Lee, "May I see you home? I'm not sure you would be safe by yourself."

"Oh yes, thank you." Hester Lee answered. "I was hoping you would. I saw Aunt Elizabeth leave awhile ago with Jessie and Josh. All the excitement must have tired her out. What do you suppose is keeping Mr. Dobbs?"

"Hard to day," Turk was sure he was fine and was having himself a time. He was probably with the noisiest bunch there was. They had planned to stay overnight and had made arrangements to sleep in their wagon at the stable.

Helping Hester Lee into the wagon, Turk was surprised to realize having her so close was making him tremble. This woman sure has a strange effect on me, he decided.

Stopping in front of the shop, Turk helped her down and commented on how much he liked the name of her shop. "I guess Canning Jar Clothiers is about the perfect name. How did you come up with it?" He asked politely.

Hester Lee's cheeks became a little pink as she answered, "I'm just partial to canning jars, I guess. Especially one that a certain very handsome young boy filled with wild flowers."

Turk was stunned. His face must have shown this as Hester Lee continued. "Years ago I'm afraid I was watching as you placed a jar of flowers on your mother's grave. You stood for a long time and when you lifted your chin and squared you shoulders and slowly walked away, you truly broke my heart." The memory caused tears to well up in her green eyes and spill over down her cheeks.

Turk touched her cheek and tried to wipe the tears away with his shaking hand.

"Please don't cry." Turk was dismayed to find his own eyes getting damp. "I can't bear to see you cry, What can I do?"

"It may help if you kiss me, John," she whispered in a small voice.

The kiss went on and on. When Turk finally raised his head and looked down into those bewitching eyes, he whispered, "I love you Hester Lee with all my heart. You have me so mixed up. I don't have any idea what's going on and I don't know what to do."

"Well, lucky for you, I do know what you should do next, Mr. John Turk. I'm afraid you are going to have to marry me."

# Chapter Twenty-Six

The excitement of the grand opening of Mayville Park was nothing compared to the excitement of the next morning. The news spread like wildfire. Hester Lee and Turk were going to get married.

Turk was trying to wake Dobbs with no luck at all. When he had come to the wagon very late last night, he was surprised to find Dobbs sleeping under the wagon. He wondered if maybe Dobbs found the scattered hay softer than the wooden wagon bed. At last Dobbs roused and rubbing his head, Turk found out the real reason for Dobbs sleeping arrangement

"I couldn't stop this dang wagon from spinning," Dobbs explained. "I figured the only way to stop it was to sleep on the ground and hang on. Now what is so important that you wake a man who might be on his deathbed?"

Turk told Dobbs the news and all that he and Hester Lee had decided. They had talked almost until dawn. Turk didn't think it would be right to have Hester Lee live so far from town and she really wanted to keep her little clothing shop. Turk didn't want to move to town, so there was a compromise. He would build a house for them on his property as close to town as possible.

"Congratulations, old buddy," Dobbs grabbed Turk in a big bear hug. "You are getting a fine young woman and she will be getting about the best man around. I am not surprised, I was starting to wonder what you were waiting for."

"That news was just the medicine I needed. I do believe I will make it now, but I bet a few of those fellers I was with last night are waking up with some aching heads this morning." Dobbs spoke in a bit more serious voice, "I realize this means I won't be seeing much of my old partner, but we will still be partners, won't we, Turk?"

"Of course," Turk answered. "I will be busy building my house, but I will help out at the post when I can. Right now I would be happy to buy you some breakfast."

"Maybe a hot cup of coffee," Dobbs said as he straightened his clothes and tired to smooth his hair. "I'm not ready for food yet."

May's place was busy. Lots of the settlers had spent the night and wanted a good breakfast before heading back to their homes. There were smiles and congratulations from many of them. May was not content with just talk. She gave Turk a big kiss and told him something surprising.

"Hester Lee was here a while ago and I am so proud that she asked me to be her maid of honor." May spoke in a way not so gushy. "It's the nicest thing that ever happened to me. I never dreamed anyone would ever consider me to be in their wedding. I did make two conditions," May held up two fingers as she explained, "First I wanted Hester Lee to make me a new dress out of the brightest shiniest pink material she could find and second, I wanted to make both of you the fanciest most spectacular wedding cake there ever was."

Turk ate his food quickly as he wanted to see Hester Lee. He was pretty sure, she wouldn't change her mind. It was hard to believe that such a beautiful woman would want to marry him.

Aunt Elizabeth and Hester Lee were busy looking at catalogues. "John, we have so much to do." Hester Lee said in that sweet voice. "I would like to make you a suit as my wedding present to you. Would you please let me do that? It would make me very happy."

Turk knew he would never be able to refuse her anything. He nodded in agreement

Aunt Elizabeth looked over at Dobbs. "Mr. Dobbs, you don't look like you are having as much fun as you were last night. I think we should sew a suit for you, too. I'm assuming you will be the best man."

"Well, I guess so. I always figured I was the best man anyway. I would appreciate a new suit of course it would be my old suit, my new suit and the last one I had made, because I never had a suit before."

Everyone had a big laugh over this. As the laughter died down, Turk reluctantly said, "We only have about two months to get lots of work done, so I guess we better get busy."

The next two months were very busy, but very happy too. Hester Lee insisted on ordering furniture for her new home. She made curtains and bed linen. She bought dishes and cooking pans. About every other day she would come to the building site with something new.

The mile from town seemed shorter each time she came. The first thing she did after the table and chairs arrived was to place a canning jar full of wildflowers on the table. Each day she came, she picked a new arrangement.

Turk and Hester Lee had so many happy talks together. They never ran out of things to say.

One day the conversation turned to a wedding ring. Turk

told Hester lee about how his mother had taken off her ring when his father deserted them.

"Do you have her ring, John?" Hester Lee asked in a soft voice. "If you do, I would love to have it for my wedding ring. It would be as though your mother would be a part of our life."

"That is so thoughtful of you." Turk answered. "Yes, I do have it, but wouldn't you rather have a new one of your own?"

"Absolutely not," she answered. "I would be proud to wear that ring. May I see it?"

The ring fit perfectly. Seeing the ring on Hester Lee's finger made Turk realize this was not a dream. It was really going to happen.

"Take this back for now, John. The next time it is on my finger, I plan to never take it off again."

Many days and many busy hours later, Dobbs and Turk are sitting on the porch of the new house.

Their new suits are hanging in the new closet along with the new boots that both men had ordered from the general store. The house was not completely finished, but definitely livable. It had to be because the big day was tomorrow.

"You do realize that after tomorrow, your whole life is changed, don't you, Turk?" Dobbs asked in a sober tone.

"I know that's true, but I cannot imagine life without Hester Lee," Turk said in an even more serious voice.

"'You never had a chance, old buddy, Hester Lee had her mind made up when she was a little girl that you were the one for her. I guess you are just lucky. I feel we are both lucky. Buying this land and our trading post and Hester Lee, doncha think we are about the two luckiest fellers around, Turk?"

Turk smiled at his old friend. "Yes, I absolutely do think so."

# Would you like to see your manuscript become a book?

If you are interested in becoming a PublishAmerica author, please submit your manuscript for possible publication to us at:

**acquisitions@publishamerica.com**

You may also mail in your manuscript to:

**PublishAmerica
PO Box 151
Frederick, MD 21705**

# www.publishamerica.com

CPSIA information can be obtained at www.ICGtesting.com
Printed in the USA
BVOW022136200212

283387BV00001B/75/P

9 781456 012557